# Billionaire Unexplained

## THE BILLIONAIRE'S OBSESSION
### Kaleb

# J. S. SCOTT

Billionaire Unexplained

Cover Photo by Wander Aguiar Photography
Proof Editing by Virginia Tesi Carey

ISBN: 979-8-884531-26-0 (Print)
ISBN: 978-1-959932-06-2 (E-Book)

# Contents

## Chapter 1

*Kaleb*

"If you're not home as soon as this snowstorm ends, Devon and I are coming to get you," my brother, Tanner, warned me the second I picked up the satellite phone in the remote cabin. "I'm not saying that you don't desperately need a break from work, but we both know that's not what you're doing at the cabin right now."

I raked a frustrated hand through my hair as I sat down on the bed in the bedroom of the cabin. Hell, I probably shouldn't have answered the phone, but there *was* a raging spring snowstorm going on outside, and I didn't want my family to be concerned about me.

I had left my home in Crystal Fork, Montana pretty abruptly a few days ago.

"I just needed a few days alone to think," I admitted to Tanner.

There was no way I was going to convince my brother that I was taking a few days off to do some fishing or rest and relax here in this remote location.

We'd just gotten back from my cousin Shelby's wedding in San Diego when I'd decided to bolt.

Tanner *knew* that wasn't a coincidence.

There was definitely a downside to being so close to my two younger brothers. We knew each other so well that they immediately knew when I was doing something out of character.

The truth was, I wasn't usually the kind of guy who left at a moment's notice to pull his head together.

I was generally the way-too-serious, eldest Remington brother who didn't know when to stop working.

"You have to stop feeling guilty about what happened to Shelby," Tanner said firmly. "We were just at her wedding, Kaleb. She's healthy and happier than she's ever been."

What my brother was saying was very true. Shelby, who was more like a little sister to me than a cousin, had just married one of my best friends in San Diego. She was ecstatically happy with Wyatt, and I was grateful that she was finally with the man she deserved.

It was just damn hard to forget how close she'd come to never seeing that wedding or a happily ever after.

All because I'd chosen work over her safety.

"It wasn't your fault, Kaleb," Tanner said like he'd been reading my thoughts. "It was six months ago. The kidnapping is in the rearview mirror for her now. Let it go."

*Easy for him to say. Tanner isn't the one who left Shelby alone in the barn and vulnerable.*

Now, every time I saw her, I was reminded that I'd failed to protect her from falling into the hands of a serial killer.

I had recurrent nightmares about the event, even though I hadn't been the one to rescue her. For a while, I'd had them nearly every night after she was rescued. As the months had gone by, they'd gotten better, but seeing her again last week had triggered a hellacious nightmare when I'd returned from her wedding.

I'd literally been a bystander in that nightmare while Shelby was being abused and murdered. It was vivid, probably triggered by being at her wedding. I'd woken up in a cold sweat, reliving that damn nightmare over and over while I was awake.

It was so bad that I'd needed to get away for a few days, and for some reason, I'd been drawn to the remote cabin I hadn't visited in a very long time.

In retrospect, maybe the remote cabin hadn't been such a great idea. It left me alone with my thoughts way too much, and the guilt of what I'd done was still eating me alive.

I'd *known* that Shelby was vulnerable, and that she had a possible stalker.

Maybe I'd only left her alone for a few minutes to finish a work call, but it had been long enough for her to get kidnapped and live out a horrifying ordeal that never should have happened.

No, she hadn't been murdered or raped, but she would have been if she hadn't gotten rescued when she did.

"It *was* my fault," I said hoarsely. "I wasn't there for her."

Just like I hadn't been there when my dad had died of a heart attack three years ago. None of us had been in Crystal Fork then. My mother had been alone until we'd been able to get back home. My brothers and I had been away on what we'd considered a very important business trip out of the country at the time.

Yeah, maybe I couldn't have predicted what had happened to my father. There had been zero warning signs that he was going to die anytime soon. But he was older, and I now regretted not spending more quality time with him.

Hell, now that I'd turned forty years old, maybe I was trying to get my priorities straight.

I'd spent all of my adult years chasing business goals. Now that I'd realized all of those ambitions, I was starting to recognize that I'd been a selfish prick.

What had happened to Shelby had been a huge wake-up call for me.

I couldn't seem to shake off the guilt I felt every time I thought about the day of her kidnapping, and how it could have so easily been avoided. It was especially difficult when I saw her in person. It reminded me of just how close we'd come to losing her to a homicidal psycho.

B. A. Scott

"Wyatt has told you a million times that Ted Young would have gotten to Shelby somehow," Tanner answered in an exasperated voice. "If not here, he would have eventually got to her back in San Diego. He was an obsessed lunatic, Kaleb. Had you been with Shelby in that barn, he probably would have just shot you and taken her. You couldn't have protected her when he had a loaded firearm. He would have done whatever it took to get to her. Hell, we all thought she was safe here at home."

"She wasn't safe," I corrected. "And bad shit can happen anywhere."

I'd learned *that* the hard way.

Maybe crime was extremely rare in Crystal Fork, but no part of the world was isolated from crazy people, not even the small Montana town I'd grown up in.

It had been my responsibility to protect my younger cousin while she was here in Montana. Wyatt had trusted me to watch out for her in his absence, and I'd failed. If it hadn't been for Wyatt's risky rescue, Shelby wouldn't have had that dream wedding we'd just attended.

"Look," Tanner replied. "I know you've always had an overinflated sense of responsibility, but you have to stop with the guilt trips or those damn nightmares are going to eat you alive. Shelby is happy. She doesn't blame you for what happened. Neither does Wyatt, and you know how protective he is. Shelby didn't take the whole stalker thing seriously, either. She knows that she should have waited a few minutes so you could go out to the barn together. None of us took the stalker situation seriously enough, Kaleb. We thought she was perfectly safe in Crystal Fork. We had no reason to believe that a serial killer was tailing her. What were the chances of that happening? You're the most rational man I know. Use some of that common sense to shake this off."

"I think I really need to get all of my priorities straight," I confessed gruffly.

I'd spent my entire adult life making work my priority.

Now that my two brothers and I were all billionaires and had found that success beyond what we'd ever believed possible, I was strangely...restless.

❧ 4 ❧

It wasn't that I didn't love my work and my business, but I felt like something important was missing.

At some point in my workaholic existence, I'd lost sight of what was important to me.

"You think?" Tanner asked drily. "We all work hard, Kaleb, but your life has revolved around KTD Remington since the moment you got out of college. We're all dedicated to KTD, but it's your entire life. There has to be life beyond work, brother."

"Yeah, well," I grumbled. "I guess I haven't figured out exactly what a more balanced life is like yet."

Family had always been important to me. I was a Remington. It was ingrained in my DNA.

Nevertheless, KTD had taken priority quite a few times when it shouldn't have been that way.

"Then figure out what those priorities are, and bring your ass back home," Tanner insisted. "Devon and I feel guilty about misleading Mom. She thinks you're somewhere on a business trip. She has no idea that you're drowning in guilt in her cabin."

Technically, the cabin I was staying in *did* belong to my mother. My dad had bought it as a retreat for the two of them over a decade ago, and they'd used it often. She had decided that the cabin now belonged to her sons because she couldn't bear to come back here after my father's death, but her name was still on the deed. And it would stay that way.

"She'd worry if she knew I *wasn't* on a business trip somewhere," I reminded Tanner.

I didn't take vacations or time off to relax.

*Ever.*

If I'd used the excuse that I wanted to get away for a few days for anything other than work, my mother would have been instantly suspicious and worried.

My brother released a long breath. "I know. That's the only reason we haven't given up your real location. She'd never buy the fact that you wanted to do some early spring fishing in the middle of nowhere during a massive snowstorm. She'd want to know exactly what's wrong with you."

I'd shared my guilt and nightmares with my brothers, but it was the last thing I wanted to reveal to my mother. She'd been through enough sadness and emotional trauma after my father's death.

"I'll be back once the storm clears," I promised.

"What in the hell possessed you to take off like that when a huge storm was coming?" Tanner questioned.

I shrugged, even though he couldn't see that action. "I didn't check the weather. It was almost sixty degrees when I left Crystal Fork."

It was a sad excuse, but it was the truth.

"Which really tells me just how eager you were to get away," Tanner observed.

My brother didn't need to remind me that it was downright idiotic to not pay attention to the weather in Montana. It could change in the blink of an eye. I was born here, and I'd lived here most of my life.

Blizzards in the springtime weren't all that unusual here.

"I'm coming back soon," I insisted. "When I left, I'd only planned on hanging out here for the weekend. The storm is extending my visit, unfortunately. All aircrafts are grounded until this blizzard passes."

There was a brief pause before Tanner finally asked hesitantly, "Why the cabin? Why now? It's been years since any of us have been there. None of us have been there since Dad died."

His question made sense. After all, I had a private jet that could take me anywhere I wanted to escape for a short time. "I'm not entirely sure," I replied honestly.

Some weird instinct had drawn me here for some reason, which sounded pretty ridiculous. It wasn't like this cabin my parents had loved was going to tell me what I needed in my life and exactly how to forgive myself for the mistakes I'd made in the past.

I'd been here for a few days, and I hadn't gotten a single answer to those questions.

A sudden sound coming from the window prompted me to get up from the bed, wondering who or what could possibly be out in this blizzard.

Most likely, it was the wind tossing something against the window, but I decided I'd better check it out.

"Hey, I have to go," I said to Tanner distractedly. "I'll call you back."

I disconnected the call without waiting for his response and dropped the phone on the bedside table.

I was surprised as I turned toward the sound I'd heard a moment ago and saw the window actually starting to rise.

*Definitely not the wind blowing things around.*

The window squeaked a little as it slowly opened.

A small backpack was suddenly flung into the room, and it hit the floor with a *thump!*

At that point, I knew I should probably be concerned about who was about to enter the room, but I was more annoyed that my peace was about to be disrupted.

One glance at the figure struggling to get inside told me that I wasn't going to have to defend myself against an unwanted intruder.

It was a smallish figure, a female, and she literally dropped through the window and collapsed on the floor.

Her teeth were chattering, and she was shivering so hard she could barely get two words out of her mouth. "N-need, h-help."

"Fuck!" I cursed as I closed the window and knelt down next to her, knowing we were a long ways away from the medical help she probably needed right now.

Honestly, even if we weren't pretty far from town at this cabin, there was no way medics were going to get through the blizzard and blocked roads to take care of this woman.

My gut twisted as she shot me a desperate look with a pair of dark, beguiling eyes before she promptly passed out on the bedroom floor.

*Fucking hell!*

I knelt down and felt for her pulse and made sure she was breathing before I started to strip off her wet jacket, a lighter garment that wasn't suited for a Montana blizzard.

*No hat.*

*No gloves.*

No real insulation from the brutal, frigid winds that were howling right outside the damn window.

What in the hell had she been thinking?

And where had she come from?

No sane person would be out in this storm right now.

As I quickly removed anything that was wet from her body, I contemplated the fact that it was entirely possible that she was out of her mind. *Literally.*

*Maybe a tourist with a death wish?*

The only problem with that theory was that we weren't exactly in a tourist area, and not that many people flooded into this part of Montana at this time of year to see the sights.

I left her undergarments on because they were only slightly damp, and quickly went to get some towels and blankets.

Her skin was ice-cold, but I knew better than to try to warm her up too fast. I wasn't a trained medical professional, but I knew enough about the outdoors and the treatment for hypothermia.

I frowned as I dried her hair quickly, and removed her glasses. She'd broken them when she'd done that swan dive headfirst through the window.

The lenses seemed to be intact, but the frames were broken.

Setting the glasses aside, I focused on my uninvited and unwanted guest as I wrapped her dry but cold body into the blankets, picked her up, and carried her to the living room.

I plopped my ass on the plush rug in front of the warm fireplace, and pulled the shivering woman into my lap, my arms tightly around her blanketed body.

Hell, this was the last thing I wanted or needed.

I also sucked at taking care of anyone, but I was all she had right now.

She stirred, but she didn't open her eyes, which led me to believe she'd probably passed out from possible exhaustion. She definitely wasn't completely unconscious.

She was small, and fighting against the storm and brutal winds outside had probably taken everything she had.

I had no idea how long she'd been lost in the wilderness.

Did she have family?

"At these temperatures, and at these windchills, hypothermia sets in fast. Especially when you're not dressed for a bad storm," he explained like he was talking to someone who wasn't quite rational. "I'll get you something warm to drink."

Despite his crankiness, he set me gently onto the rug before he rose to go to the kitchen.

God, he was testy, but his home and his assistance were saving my life, so I wasn't about to complain.

I wouldn't be all that happy if someone dropped into my place through the window, either.

Besides, a warm drink sounded heavenly at the moment, even if it wasn't the salted caramel latte I'd practically kill for right now.

I wrapped the blanket tighter around me, grateful to be indoors.

My reluctant host apparently didn't know who I was, which was an enormous relief.

I'd come here to escape from the things that had happened in California, and I'd prefer that the owner of this cabin didn't know exactly who had crashed in on his solitude.

I'd come to Montana because it had always been a peaceful, happy place for me, which were two things I needed to regain my sanity.

My breath caught when my gorgeous host walked back into the room with a mug in his hand.

The man was ridiculously handsome, and his sheer size seemed to suck all the air from the living room.

I hated the way I couldn't manage to pull my gaze away from those mesmerizing green eyes of his that surveyed me carefully as he handed me the mug.

The poor guy was obviously wary. Really, could I blame him? Only an idiot would be outdoors in this horrible storm.

Maybe I should be more cautious, too, but for some weird reason, I wasn't afraid of him. Probably because he had apparently been trying to save me from my own stupidity.

*Dammit!* Everything about him was intriguing, and the last thing I needed was to be stuck with a man who I couldn't stop ogling like a twitterpated teenager. He was dressed like a lumberjack in jeans and a red flannel shirt, but he spoke in a no-nonsense, low baritone that sounded somewhat refined and educated to me. He had scruff on his face that probably hadn't seen a razor in the last few days, but even *that* was kind of sexy.

"I told you my name," I pointed out as he handed me the mug. "What's yours?"

I couldn't keep thinking of him as *my grumpy but very sexy host.*

"Kaleb," he said shortly as he sat down on the rug next to me. "Now, would you care to explain to me exactly what you're doing here. If you got stuck in the driveway, you were obviously heading here in the first place."

He didn't give me any other information, but I wasn't about to reveal my identity, either, so I wasn't about to criticize his abruptness or his bossiness.

I took a sip of the hot chocolate and sighed before I replied. "I wasn't headed to your place. I was headed to a rental home. I ended up here instead. I didn't realize this was the wrong place until I got closer to the cabin. The place I was looking for is a lot more contemporary. It's not a log home."

Kaleb nodded. "You probably missed the neighbor's driveway because of the storm. There's a place a few miles back that does vacation rentals sometimes, but people generally only want to stay this remote in the summer."

I nearly choked on my hot chocolate. "Your only neighbor lives a few miles away? How is that still considered a neighbor?"

He shrugged. "This cabin has seven or eight hundred acres. That makes them close to the property line."

I shot him a small smile. He was right. I'd just forgotten how vast Montana could be in remote places like this. "What do you do with eight hundred acres in this area?"

"This is prime hunting land," he said vaguely.

"So you're here to hunt?" I asked curiously.

God, dragging any information out of this stoic man was almost impossible.

There were mysteries about Kaleb that I really wanted to solve.

I didn't take offense because I was getting used to his less than friendly tone.

I was beginning to realize that he probably always sounded disgruntled and cynical.

"It was warm when I got into Montana," I explained. "This storm seemed to come out of nowhere as I was driving here."

"You didn't check the weather? You're a native Montanan."

"I didn't," I admitted. "I was distracted."

He smirked ruefully. "Okay, then I'm going to admit that I didn't check the weather before I came here, either, for the same reason. Because we were both careless, I think we're stuck here together for a while."

"And are you a native?" I questioned in a teasing voice.

"Yep," he replied.

I really loved the way he could admit to being human and making mistakes. It was something I didn't see often in my world.

"I take it you don't live here in this area all the time," I commented, not sure how much I could say without stepping into territory that was too personal.

He shook his head. "I don't. This was a place my parents came to when they wanted to get away before my father died. My dad hunted here, and my mother loved the area and the scenery. I actually haven't been here in a long time. I wasn't planning on staying long. I live in a small town called Crystal Fork. It's near Billings."

"Too painful?" I asked sadly.

He didn't deny it. "Yeah. How did you know?"

I swallowed hard and willed the tears not to flow. "Let's just say I know something about losing the people you love. I'm sorry about your dad."

He acknowledged my words of sympathy with a quick nod. "It's been three years now. I guess I felt like it was time to come back here."

He hadn't said much, but it was the first really personal information he'd shared.

"It's a beautiful cabin," I told him.

*B. A. Scott*

The place was small, but obviously well loved. Maybe it was prime hunting land, but it didn't look like a typical hunting cabin. Beautiful landscapes covered the walls, and the furniture looked like it was chosen because it was attractive and comfortable. We were sitting in front of the big, stone fireplace in an open living room. Beyond, I could see a nice kitchen with what appeared to be all the modern conveniences. Across the room, there was a door, which probably went to the bedroom I'd literally dropped into a while ago.

Okay, I hadn't seen much of the bedroom before I'd passed out, but the entire place definitely had a woman's touch.

I reached out my hand and ran it across the beautiful coffee table behind us. It looked like it was handcrafted. "Did your father make this?" I asked softly. "It's a work of art."

"I made that years ago from reclaimed barn wood," he told me. "Dad did the bookshelves and the furniture in the bedroom. There's a workshop out in the heated garage. Working with wood was something we both enjoyed doing."

I wanted to ask if he made furniture for a living. He certainly had the talent to make it a profession. But asking about careers would probably be crossing the line.

Since neither one of us really wanted to talk about why we were here, I felt like we had an unspoken agreement not to ask super personal questions.

"It's amazing workmanship," I observed as I looked at the bookshelves against the wall.

"Thanks," he said as he shot me a questioning look. "Can you see everything okay without your glasses? The frames were broken when you hit the floor in the bedroom."

*Damn!* I'd forgotten about the glasses. "I'm wearing contacts," I told him. "The glasses were in my backpack. I put them on to try to protect my eyes from the wind."

It was probably the dumbest excuse on the planet. Obviously, I would have problems seeing if I put prescription glasses on over my prescription contacts, and judging by his guarded expression, he knew it.

"Let me guess. The lenses of those glasses are clear glass?" he asked quietly.

"Yes," I answered truthfully. "Please don't ask me why."

I didn't want to lie to Kaleb. He was my rescuer. But I also didn't feel like explaining why I was trying to disguise myself, either.

The room was quiet for a few moments other than the crackling of the fire as his gaze searched my face.

"Are you sure you're not hiding from someone, Anna? Or are you in some kind of trouble?" he finally questioned gravely.

He sounded disappointed, and for some reason, I hated that.

I slowly shook my head as I looked away from his probing gaze. "No. No one is chasing me, and I'm not in trouble legally or anything. There's just some things I don't want to talk about."

He reached out, gently took my chin, and turned my eyes to his again. "I get it. There are things I don't want to talk about, either. Keep your secrets for now, Anna, and I'll keep mine. We're stuck here together, so it's impossible for us not to talk to each other. No lies. If there's something we don't want to discuss, we just say so—like you just did. We're going to have to trust each other while we're here. Does that sound fair?"

Something warm spread through my belly as our gazes stayed locked for what seemed like forever.

Once again, I wanted to break down and tell him everything. I wanted to talk to someone I trusted, but I couldn't. He might be a stranger who didn't feel like a stranger to me, but I wasn't a naïve woman. I'd lived in Los Angeles for a long time.

"Sounds like a deal," I said lightly, knowing I had no choice but to trust Kaleb with my safety right now.

However, it would be crazy for me to spill my guts to a hot stranger in the Montana wilderness just because he *felt* like a safe place to me for some unknown reason.

There was absolutely no reason why we couldn't just be casual acquaintances until we could get the hell out of this cabin and back to civilization again.

# Chapter 3

*Kaleb*

"I *am not* going to press her for more information," I muttered to myself as I stirred the beef stew on the stove. "The last thing I need is to get involved in her life, even if I could convince her to trust me."

I'd spent the last ten minutes trying to convince myself that Anna was a stranger, and it was none of my damn business what secrets she was hiding.

I now knew that she wasn't crazy.

I also believed that she was telling me the truth about not running from the law or a stalker.

That was all that mattered, right?

She wasn't so insane that she'd kill me while I was sleeping, and no one was going to snatch her when I wasn't looking.

We'd be pleasant to each other while we were stuck together.

That was all.

The problem was, I wanted to know what was bothering her so much that she'd left her life in California for the remote wilderness of Montana.

She was obviously an intelligent woman.

And fuck knew she was attractive.

Wasn't there someone she wanted to be with in California if she had problems that were getting to her?

*Christ!* I *didn't* need to know the answer to that.

She was a goddamn stranger to me, yet I still wondered...

Anna was beautiful, intelligent, and seemingly kind, so it was hard to believe she didn't have someone in her life that she could run to instead of coming here alone.

Unfortunately, I *was* physically attracted to her. If she thought that wearing glasses made her less noticeable, she was wrong. But I was forty years old, not a horny teenager. I could control my dick when a beautiful woman was nearby. That had never been an issue for me before.

Yeah, I'd had a few relationships in the past, but they were generally short-lived because I was constantly consumed by my company and work.

After a while, I'd stopped trying to make an intimate partnership work.

I'd decided a long time ago that hookups with women my age who were also married to their careers worked out better for me, and I was okay with that.

It was easier and less complicated.

That was probably why I was surprised that I *wanted* to know more about Anna and what was happening in her life.

The woman had *complicated* written all over her, and I didn't do complicated in my personal life. I actually had no personal life other than my family.

"Leave this situation alone, asshole," I grumbled to myself as I checked the biscuits in the oven.

I wasn't a culinary genius, but I could manage to put a simple meal together. My mother had refused to raise boys who couldn't take care of themselves.

The cabin caretaker had stocked the place well, so most of my choices were heat-and-eat, which worked out fine for me since I didn't do anything fancy.

J. A. Scott

"Did I hear you talking to yourself?" Anna asked as she strolled into the kitchen.

Hell, I'd forgotten that we were in a small cabin and that she could probably hear me from the bedroom.

I turned to see her smiling, her hair still damp from the shower. Every firm affirmation I'd just made to myself about her being a stranger flew right out of my brain.

It was like I couldn't get a rational thought in my head when she was this damn close.

It wasn't just the fact that she was beautiful.

There was something about Anna that made me want to know everything about her, even though it was none of my business.

"Bad habit," I said, turning away from her warm smile and teasing eyes.

I pulled the biscuits out of the oven and turned down the heat on the stew.

"Can I help?" she asked softly. "I'm sorry I left you to cook dinner, but I really needed a hot shower. I was traveling most of the day, and that trek down your endless driveway worked up a sweat. I'm sure I didn't smell very good."

I hadn't noticed.

She'd smelled fine to me.

Maybe too good.

"I can handle heating up stew and biscuits," I replied, waving toward the small table in the kitchen. "Have a seat. I'm actually surprised that you're still standing after nearly freezing to death."

"I feel okay," she insisted as she looked around the kitchen. "I'm just really exhausted."

That wasn't surprising after the day she'd had.

Honestly, she did look like she was wiped out, but I didn't think the dark circles under her eyes were from trekking down the long driveway in the cold.

I dished up the stew and put a few biscuits on a plate as Anna put a gentle hand on the fancy coffee maker my mother adored.

"I have the exact same model," she said adoringly as her hand stroked over the machine. "It makes the best salted caramel latte out there."

I put the plate with the biscuits and our bowls of stew on the table and then stepped next to her to open the cupboard. "Help yourself. I don't use it for anything other than strong coffee, but I think I'm stocked to make almost anything."

She let out an audible gasp as she looked at all the syrups and coffee accessories. "Oh, my God, you do have everything."

I had no idea what she needed to make that salted caramel coffee thing, but the longing note in her voice when she'd talked about it made me hope the supplies were there to make it.

She opened the fridge, and when she saw the milk, she sounded almost giddy as she added, "I can make almost any latte we want. I could hug you right now. I'll make us one after dinner."

Okay, so she was a woman who really loved her coffee. I could respect that.

"I'm pretty much a strong, black coffee drinker only. Mom is the one who likes the fancy coffee drinks. A caretaker did the stocking."

I really wanted to tell her that I'd take that damn hug anyway, but I didn't. Getting that close to Anna would be a very bad idea.

She frowned as she sat down at the table. "Seriously? Who doesn't love a good latte? I'm kind of an addict."

"You drink coffee this late?" I asked as I sat and dug into the stew. It was getting close to midnight.

"Always," she said between bites. "I tend to work late sometimes. When I go to bed, I'm exhausted. Caffeine doesn't bother me. Does it bother you?"

I shook my head. I slammed coffee late, just like her, to stay awake when I was working late, which was most of the time. "Are you asking that because I'm over forty now?" I joked.

She rolled her eyes as she continued to wolf down her food. She wasn't a dainty, slow eater, which I found interesting. I got the impression that she had to grab food whenever she could because I ate the same way.

"You aren't old," she admonished. "Caffeine bothers a lot of people. It's never been an issue for me. My life is a little...crazy."

"Crazy how?" I asked carefully.

I wasn't sure if she'd answer. I was asking for details that we'd agreed not to talk about.

"It's unconventional," she explained readily. "I work weird hours sometimes. I don't really want to talk about my job, but let's just say that I don't have a nine-to-five occupation."

Since I could relate to that, I answered, "I don't want to talk about my job, but I don't have normal hours, either."

"I thought maybe you were a furniture maker," she mused after she had polished off the last biscuit.

"I'm not," I confessed. "Woodworking is a hobby, and it's not one that I've been able to indulge in for a long time."

Truthfully, I didn't have hobbies anymore. I'd given those up for KTD a long time ago.

She held up her hand. "I'm not going to ask what you do since neither of us wants to talk about work. Are you totally against personal questions of any kind?"

I eyed her cautiously. "How personal?"

She hopped up and grabbed two more biscuits from the tray because the plate was empty. She dropped one on a napkin next to my bowl as she sat back down and started to eat the other one. "My hands are clean. I hope you're not a germaphobe. If you are, I'm really sorry."

Her expression was genuinely contrite, which was pretty adorable. So I picked up the biscuit and started to devour it.

Now that she was recovered, I could tell that she was a little high-strung, but not in a bad way.

In fact, she was fascinating, and I felt like I was getting caught up in her infectious spirit.

And I definitely was *not* an upbeat guy most of the time.

She went back to her original topic. "Personal questions like—are you married, and do you have any kids? Maybe they're dumb questions. If you were married, you'd probably be here with your family, right?"

"I'm not married. Never have been, and I don't have kids," I told her. I was fine with those kinds of personal questions because I wanted to ask her the same thing. "You?"

"Same," she said with a sigh. "It's not that I don't want those things, but it's never worked out for me. I'm pretty sure there is no Mr. Right for me."

"You don't know that," I scoffed. "You're still young, and it sounds like you're career focused."

"It's not just that," she said as she placed her spoon in her empty bowl. "I'm...different. I can't explain that without getting too personal."

Oh hell, now I was really intrigued, but I'd promised that I wasn't going to push her to tell me things she didn't want to talk about. "You seem pretty normal to me."

She beamed at me. "Thanks. Do you want another biscuit?"

"I'm good," I answered.

"I'm stuffed," she said as she put a hand on her flat belly. "I'll do the dishes."

I helped her by carrying the plate and bowls to the dishwasher. Since there wasn't much to clean up, it only took a few minutes.

"Do you mind?" she asked hopefully as she glanced at the coffee maker once we'd put the last utensil in the dishwasher.

"Knock yourself out," I said, amused.

I'd never seen a woman get so excited over such a small thing.

I grabbed a beer for myself from the fridge, and refused the coffee she offered to make me. I watched her make her coffee like a skilled barista.

I balked as I saw her add a dash of salt to her creation. "Salt in your coffee?" I questioned.

"Don't knock it until you try it," she shot back. "It's a salted caramel latte. It wouldn't taste right without it, and it's addictive."

I shot her a skeptical look, but she sipped the coffee like it was a drink from the gods.

The satisfied look on her face got me hard almost immediately.

She looked like a woman who had just had multiple orgasms.

*Fuck!* I was almost jealous because I hadn't put that expression on her face myself.

What in the hell was wrong with me?

"Good?" I asked hoarsely.

"Orgasmic," she said with a long, euphoric sigh.

I almost spit a gulp of beer out of my mouth.

Yeah, it was a common expression, but those words coming from her mouth when I was just thinking about the same thing was a little uncomfortable.

Disgusted with myself, I forced that gulp of beer down my throat and went to look out the kitchen window. The storm was still raging outside. I couldn't see much because it was dark, but the wind was howling like crazy.

"I take it we're going to sleep together," Anna said cheerily.

I turned abruptly, only to see her smiling sweetly at me.

*Christ!* I needed to get my mind out of the gutter.

She shrugged. "I don't see another bedroom, and you have a big bed."

"I'll take the couch," I said immediately.

There was no way in hell that I could sleep in the same bed with Anna.

"No, you won't," she insisted as she eyed me from head to toe. "You'd never fit, but I can sleep on the couch if you want."

"Not happening," I informed her roughly. I was not putting her on the couch. It was comfortable enough to sit on, but sleeping on it was almost impossible. She was exhausted, and she'd never get a good night's sleep.

There was a small apartment over the big, detached garage. My brothers and I had bunked there a few times when my dad had first bought the cabin, but my parents had started using it for storage when we'd decided it was more comfortable to stay in town on our visits. I'd checked it out earlier in my stay, and it was full. I wasn't even sure those bunk beds were in there anymore.

Sleeping together was a logical solution, and I was usually a rational guy.

The bed was a king.

There was plenty of space for both of us.

"Don't worry," she said breezily. "I trust you, and it makes sense."

I tossed back the last of my beer. It was a good thing that she trusted me, because when it came to Anna, I wasn't so sure I trusted myself.

# Chapter 4

*Anna*

"Kaleb, are you still awake?" I asked softly.

I was thoroughly exhausted, but I couldn't sleep.

Judging by the way he was breathing and his restlessness, I didn't think Kaleb was asleep, either.

My pajamas were in my suitcase in my stranded vehicle, so he'd generously given up a T-shirt for me to sleep in.

He'd been on his side of the bed when I'd come out of the bathroom.

I'd barely gotten a chance to notice that he had a droolworthy bare chest before he'd turned off the lights.

"Yeah," he admitted in a husky voice. "You can't sleep? Are you cold? This place runs on solar with a generator backup. In weather like this, it gets a little chilly sometimes."

Kaleb's big, muscular body threw off enough heat to warm up the entire cabin.

I wasn't cold.

I was an emotional mess.

It was my ruminating thoughts that were keeping me awake right now.

"I'm warm enough," I answered. "Sometimes I think too much when it's this quiet and dark."

"Then talk to me," he encouraged in a voice so deep and sincere that I almost fell apart.

God, I wanted to talk to someone. I felt so alone that it was tearing me apart.

Even though Kaleb was almost a stranger to me, he *felt* like a safe place to vent the emotions that were ripping me up inside.

Maybe I couldn't tell him everything, but maybe I could share some things...

It was risky, but with Kaleb, I was willing to take that risk.

I didn't know much about him, but I felt oddly comfortable with him, even though he *was* ridiculously attractive.

"I don't have any siblings, do you?" I asked.

"I have two younger brothers that make me crazy sometimes, but I couldn't imagine not having them in my life."

I took a deep breath. "I don't have any other family, and my parents died six months ago. It was assumed at first that it was a murder and suicide."

Kaleb reached out and felt around until he found my hand, and I clasped it like it was a lifeline.

"Fuck! I'm so damn sorry. It makes sense that you wanted to escape from that for a while," he said in a raspy, agitated voice. "It's hard enough to lose one parent. I can't imagine losing both at one time, and not having any family there to support you. If you don't want to talk about it, I understand, but I'm a very sympathetic ear right now if you do."

"I want to," I whispered as tears of sorrow and confusion started to roll down my cheeks.

Honestly, I needed to talk about it with someone other than a grief counselor. Kaleb had mentioned that he'd lost his father, so I was pretty sure he'd understand how I felt.

He was silent, but I knew he was waiting until I felt comfortable enough to speak.

"I was struggling with their deaths after it happened," I confessed. "A murder/suicide just didn't make sense to me. My parents adored each other, and I thought they were incredibly happy. They were both older when I was born, so they were blissfully retired in Newport Beach so they could stay reasonably close to me. They both loved the water. They went sailing every single day. I tortured myself with the knowledge that I was their only child, and I'd obviously missed the fact that my dad was depressed. He had the gun beside him, so everyone thought that he killed my mother and then shot himself. I was still trying to work through all that guilt about not seeing a single warning sign when a detective came to me two days before I left California. He told me that they were still investigating the case because the whole theory of how they died didn't make sense to him, either. The murder/suicide explanation also didn't match the forensic evidence. He thinks they were both murdered, Kaleb."

I tried not to release the sob of anguish that had welled up in my throat, but I failed miserably.

The sound left my body like I was a wounded animal in pain.

Kaleb swiftly wrapped a strong arm around my waist and pulled me to him, then wrapped his strong arms around my body in a protective embrace.

"Let it all go, Anna," Kaleb said roughly against my hair as I sobbed my heart out. "If you keep it all inside, it will eat you alive."

His words somehow allowed me to release all of the pain and sorrow that I'd been holding inside me for a very long time.

I wasn't sure how long we stayed like that, him holding me, and me sobbing like my world was ending.

In some ways, my world *had* ended that horrible day I'd lost my parents.

Sometimes I felt so alone that I couldn't bear the emptiness inside me.

Maybe I was well into adulthood, but I'd lost the only close family members I had, and the two people who'd loved me unconditionally simply because I was their daughter.

I hadn't really cried like this since I'd first heard about my parents' deaths. It was probably only possible for me to cry like this now because I'd instinctively trusted Kaleb since the very beginning.

And I wasn't normally a very trusting soul.

"I'm sorry," I said in a tremulous voice as I rested my head against his shoulder once the tsunami of sobs had finally stopped. "You really don't need to be burdened with my personal business. I know we agreed to keep things kind of impersonal."

"I'm making it *my* business, too," he said gruffly. "What happened that sent you to Montana, Anna? Fuck knows I understand why you needed to get away, but why not right after it happened?"

He might think the whole story was a little weird. I still didn't completely know the answer to that question myself.

"I'm not sure," I admitted. "I was depressed after it happened, but I was still functioning. It wasn't until the detective told me that my parents were murdered that I had a total breakdown, Kaleb. It wasn't an uncontrollable crying sort of meltdown like this one. I just... totally lost it. It was right after a work event. I'm not even sure how I made it through that event, but afterwards, I couldn't even function. I couldn't work anymore. I felt like I'd reached the limit of what I could handle emotionally. I can't really explain what happened. I just had to get away somewhere quiet so I could think and work through this. I just wasn't functional in the real world anymore."

"What about your friends?" he asked gently.

"This might sound pathetic, but I don't have a lot of real friends. I mostly have what could be called work colleagues. My best friend, Kim, owns a health and beauty salon in Los Angeles. She wanted to come with me to Montana, but I refused. She's got her own life and a family in Los Angeles. She's one of the two people who knows where I'm holed up right now. She's going to be frantic because I haven't called her, but my cell service is sketchy. I couldn't get her on the phone."

Kaleb stroked a comforting hand over my hair. "My cell phone coverage sucks, too, but I have a satellite phone. You can call her tomorrow."

"Now you probably think I'm crazy," I said hesitantly. "I used work as a distraction after it first happened, but learning that they were murdered put me over the edge. Work wasn't distracting me anymore. I just stopped functioning rationally. I barely knew my own name."

"I get it, and I don't think you're crazy," Kaleb said in a low, soothing voice that calmed me. "I tried that whole distracting myself with work thing myself when my dad died. In some ways, I was in denial for a long time. I think it's pretty normal to try to find something that stops those racing thoughts and the guilt that inevitably seems to come with it when someone we love dies suddenly like that. Who's the other person who knows where you are right now?"

"The police detective who's handling my mom and dad's case. I need to know if they arrest someone. They aren't telling me a lot because they're still investigating. I wanted to help them, but I can't think of anyone who truly disliked my mom and dad. None of this makes any sense. Why them? They don't have any enemies," I said solemnly.

"Don't make yourself crazy trying to figure out who did it," Kaleb advised gently. "That's something the police need to handle. It's their job."

I let out a long sigh. "I can't seem to stop thinking about it. We were pretty close. I was an only child. They always supported me a hundred percent. They shouldn't have died that way. I keep wondering if they suffered. What their last moments were like. God, they were probably so scared. All of those things haunt me right now."

"Also normal," Kaleb informed me.

"I don't feel normal," I said drily. "I feel like a crazy woman. I can't do my job anymore, and my work has always been my entire life."

"I have to admit that I feel like a hypocrite for saying this because my work life is the same way. Work has been my entire life, too," Kaleb replied. "However, work isn't always a great escape from things that are eating at you. It might delay reality, but those feelings are going to work their way to the surface, eventually."

Why did it sound like he was speaking from experience? "Are you here to try to deal with something painful, too? Is that why you're here at this cabin right now?" I asked.

I knew I was getting personal, but I didn't care. I'd just spilled out a lot of the things that were bothering me.

He answered without hesitation. "Yes. But we're talking about you right now. It's nothing as traumatic as what you've been through."

"Tell me," I begged. "Maybe it will make me feel more normal. I've spilt my guts to you."

He was silent for a moment before he spoke somewhat reluctantly. "I already mentioned that my female cousin had a stalker. Her name is Shelby. She's more like a little sister to me than a cousin. She's now married to Wyatt, one of my best friends, and living happily in San Diego. During that stalking, she came to Montana to visit. I knew it was possible that she was in danger. Her home in San Diego had been broken into weeks before she came here to Montana, but nothing odd had happened since that break-in. My brothers and I were careful. We kept a close eye on her, but I let my guard down one day. We were going to go riding. I stayed in the house for a few minutes to finish a work call while she headed to the barn. In those few minutes that she wasn't in my sight, she was kidnapped by a serial killer who was obsessed with her. She was eventually rescued before he had a chance to rape and kill her, but she went through hell because I couldn't leave work behind to prioritize her safety. I guess I'm here to get my priorities straight. I wasn't home when my father died suddenly of a heart attack three years ago, either. I was out of the country...working."

My heart ached because I could hear the guilt in his tone, and I was extremely familiar with that particular emotion. I could also sense that guilt because even though our circumstances were different, we were both struggling with the same emotions. "Neither of those things were your fault, Kaleb. Sometimes things just...happen."

"Have you really been able to convince yourself that's true?" he asked. "I think there's a whole lot of guilt and self-blame flying around in this room right now."

His question was more thoughtful than accusatory. If anything, he was mocking himself and not me.

"I haven't," I confessed. "But I know logically that it's true. Unfortunately, sometimes logic and emotions don't match up. I can't explain how I feel. I know it doesn't make sense, but I can't rationalize those emotions away, even though they aren't logical."

"Ditto," he answered wryly as he tightened his arms around me protectively.

I allowed myself to totally relax in his sheltering embrace. For the first time in months, I felt safe and understood.

"If you want to have a good cry, feel free," I teased. "It might make you feel better. I think it helped me."

"I think I'll pass," he said in a throaty, amused voice. "But I'm more than happy to lend you a shoulder to cry on anytime you like."

"I really hate the fact that I needed that," I confessed. "I'm generally not the type of woman that cries all over someone I hardly know."

"I know that," he said simply. "But I'm here for you, Anna. You've been through hell. I can't say I totally understand all that you've been through, but I think you need someone else you can trust right now. I'm going to be that person for you."

Relief flooded over my body.

He was right.

I needed someone to lean on right now, and Kaleb was the only person I'd let into my head for a long time.

I wasn't quite sure why I trusted that he wouldn't judge me or my craziness, but he'd accepted how I felt without question.

He made me feel…normal.

"Why?" I whispered next to his ear. "I'm a virtual stranger to you."

"I don't know," he said earnestly.

I didn't push for an answer. There was some kind of connection between the two of us that was definitely *not* logical. And for once, I wasn't going to question those feelings.

"Maybe you need me right now, too," I mused. "Maybe we can help each other."

I got the feeling that Kaleb wasn't the kind of guy to open up to anyone, but we could talk.

We understood each other because we were struggling with regrets about our pasts.

Obviously we couldn't heal each other's wounds in a few days, but it felt good that we could be open and honest with each other about why we were here in the Montana wilderness right now.

He'd probably never know how much it meant to me that he accepted exactly who I was and what I was feeling without knowing my true identity.

I was just Anna to him, the woman he was getting to know without the outside world intruding into our space.

He chuckled a little before he finally replied. "I'm not usually an open book to anyone, but I think maybe you're right. I think you might be exactly what I need."

## Chapter 5

*Kaleb*

"Full house!" Anna said triumphantly the following afternoon as she laid her cards down on the table.

Her dark eyes sparkled as she looked at me, and for some strange reason I didn't want to pop her bubble of delight, but...

I laid my cards on the table. "Four of a kind."

She glared at me after looking at my hand, which I shouldn't find adorable, but I did.

"Impossible!" she said as she shook her head. "You're dealing. Did you stack the deck or what? Every time I have a good hand, you beat it. Who has that kind of luck all the time?"

I grinned at her as I picked up the cards. I'd been in the small blind position, so I *had* been dealing this time.

"Not all the time," I corrected. "You've pulled out some good hands."

"And you usually manage to find a hand higher than mine," she mumbled unhappily.

I hadn't cheated, even though my brothers and I had tried to pull one over on each other during a few of our poker games in the past.

Had it been easy controlling my dick when I'd had her half-naked body against me all night? No. No, it wasn't. But my protective instinct toward her was stronger than my lust at the moment.

She needed someone after all she'd been through, and I was going to be that someone she could talk to, even if it killed me.

Hell, I wanted her. There probably wasn't a healthy, single male on Earth who wouldn't. But I also really...liked her.

I was certain that my physical attraction to her wasn't reciprocated, which made it a lot easier to keep my dick in check.

"You look different without your scruffy face," she commented casually as she rose from the small table and made a beeline for the coffee machine.

Anna had carefully put away the cards and chips. Obviously, she was done with the poker session.

I ran a hand over the smooth skin of my face. I'd finally shaved after I'd gotten out of the shower this morning, and I probably did look different. I hadn't put a razor to my face since I'd arrived at the cabin.

I was starting to get used to Anna saying the first thing that came to her mind without hesitation.

Honestly, I liked it, and I was starting to appreciate being treated like a normal person.

Other than my family and close friends, most people were standoffish around me, like they had to watch everything they said to me.

Generally, I was guarded because I'd been burnt too many times in the past by people I thought were friends or intimate partners.

It was almost impossible to stay distant with Anna.

She said exactly what she thought, and expected me to answer however I wanted.

She probably had no idea that interacting with someone this way was a novelty for me.

"Do I look less scary than I did yesterday?" I asked.

She shook her head, her attention focused on her coffee creation. "No. You've never looked scary. Today, you just look...different. Your green eyes are too warm to be frightening."

I nearly laughed at her comment. My eyes were probably warm because I found her so fucking attractive.

"Would it surprise you if I told you that most people who don't know me well are terrified of me?" I asked.

I'd perfected the art of intimidation with my business adversaries over the years.

She picked up the two coffees she'd created and set one in front of me. She'd made me one this morning, and it was surprisingly good, even with that dash of salt on top.

Anna tilted her head as she surveyed me earnestly. "No, that wouldn't surprise me. I think you probably try to keep people at a distance, and you're a big, gruff kind of man on the surface. You're also extremely intelligent, which probably intimidates most people."

I frowned at her. "But you're not intimidated?"

She flashed me a sly smile that made my dick hard all over again.

"Nope," she answered as she plopped her gorgeous ass in the chair across from me. "You might be surprised by how many people I stand up to on a daily basis. Some people find me intimidating, too, but I'm actually not. I'm just used to fighting for what I want. I'm not usually the kind of woman who does stupid things, breaks into houses, or blubbers like a child on an unfamiliar shoulder. Most people don't know me at all, Kaleb. Sometimes I think it's easier if they don't."

I shrugged. "Being a mystery makes it less easy to get taken advantage of by people who aren't looking out for your best interests."

"Exactly," she said wholeheartedly. "I'm in a vicious profession. It's not possible for me to wear my heart on my sleeve. I'd get crushed in a heartbeat."

*Shit!* We really did have a lot in common. Although I was dying to know what she did for a living, I knew I couldn't ask. "Same here," I echoed.

She toyed with the handle of her mug for a moment before she finally spoke. "I know we agreed not to discuss our professions, but I'm almost sure that you're some kind of businessman. And I think I'd really hate to be your adversary."

I didn't contradict her since she was correct. I could be a major asshole when I was trying to get what I wanted for KTD. "Why?" I questioned, wanting to hear what she had to say.

She frowned. "I'm not sure I'd like that part of you as much as I like the Kaleb I know right now."

"I'm not sure you would, either," I admitted bluntly.

I bought out companies that were often in trouble. I was the hard-nosed destroyer of plenty of hopes and dreams during that process.

"Lawyer?" she asked like she was hoping I'd say that I wasn't.

"Nope," I said obligingly after I took a sip of the coffee she'd made.

"Thank God," she replied with obvious relief.

I smirked. "You obviously don't like lawyers."

"They're necessary," she said as she wrinkled her nose. "But I can't say I've ever met one that I honestly liked. In my world, they're always laser focused on getting what they want."

"Well, lucky for you that I'm not an attorney."

"But you're educated," she stated firmly.

"I went to Harvard," I readily admitted.

She folded her arms across her gorgeous breasts. "I knew it. You sound like an Ivy League guy sometimes."

"Is that a problem for you?" I asked grumpily.

She shook her head. "Not at all. Getting an Ivy League degree is a huge achievement, but I can hold my own, even though I never made it to college after high school."

Okay, now I was really curious. She was extremely bright and unnervingly perceptive. Judging from her previous comments about her work and her intelligence, I'd assumed she was in some kind of highly specialized work that required a higher education. "Was college in your plans after high school?"

"Yeah," she said wistfully. "But plans change. I took an opportunity that could be very lucrative instead of going to college. My parents barely made ends meet, and I had to make the practical choice."

If her parents had been happily retired in Newport Beach, she had obviously made the right decision. I doubted that they'd suddenly come into a lot of money on their own, and it was an expensive place to retire.

"No regrets? Everything worked out for you without college?" I asked carefully.

She smiled. "No regrets. I may not be a college grad, but I read voraciously when I'm not working. I don't think you ever stop learning. What about you? I'm going to assume that your expensive degree made you pretty successful. Are you happy with all of your life decisions?"

I knew that college wasn't everything. It was a huge boost toward success, but I'd known plenty of college grads who were total idiots without a lick of common sense.

"For the most part, yes," I explained. "I'm successful. I have an amazing family and some good friends."

"I hear a 'but' in there somewhere," she prompted. "Do you ever feel like something is missing?"

"Not until recently," I shared.

"I get it," she commiserated. "I think once you reach a certain age and level of success, you start thinking about the things you've sacrificed to get there. Success is a double-edged sword. It has both good and bad consequences sometimes, Kaleb. Especially if you've chased that success without anything else good in your life."

*Damn!* She was incredibly perceptive, and she was also right.

"You have to stop blaming yourself for what happened to Shelby and for not being home when your father died," she advised wisely. "Spend more time with the people you care about because you really want to be more present in their lives now. Don't regret the choices you made in the past. It's made you who you are today. I have a very hard time believing you've ever disappointed your family, but if you want to stop working like a madman now, you can change that. Priorities change in different phases of our lives, right? I wish I had spent a lot more time with my parents, but I never thought I wouldn't have time to do that in the future. I never, not for a moment, ever considered that they could be gone in a heartbeat. Maybe none of us do until it happens to us."

"I should have learned that lesson when my dad died," I said hoarsely. "In some ways, I guess I did. I spend far more time with my mom than I used to before he died. I don't travel as much anymore, and I actually have dinner at her house pretty often."

"So you've made some life changes," she observed. "Cut yourself a break, Kaleb. You're a strong man, but you aren't superhuman. Just admit there was no possible way you could have foreseen your father's death or your cousin's abduction. If you could have, you would have moved mountains to be there for them. I know you would have."

Would I have been there for them if I had known what the future held? Hell yes, I would have. "Maybe I'm just pissed that I didn't know," I rumbled.

She raised a brow. "Are you psychic? I know I'm not. I'm pissed that I didn't know what would happen to my parents, either, but I'm trying to work on that and my guilt about not being there. I do know that they knew how much I loved them, and I know they loved me. I'm willing to bet that your dad knew that, too. And I'm sure Shelby knows how much you care about her. No one expects you to be perfect. Most of us just want to be loved," she said softly.

"Don't try to tell me that you don't expect a lot from yourself," I said unhappily.

"Oh, I do," she readily admitted. "And that expectation of perfection crushed me. I tried until I ended up in a total meltdown because of it. I guess that's why I feel like I can give some advice on the topic. I'm an expert on expecting myself to be perfect."

Unable to stop myself, I reached across the table, snagged her around the waist and pulled her to my side and into my lap.

It wasn't something a friend might do, but I didn't give a shit.

It nearly killed me to think about Anna trying to be strong alone when her whole world had collapsed around her.

She might be a champion at hiding her pain most of the time, but I could feel her vulnerability and loneliness, and it ate my guts out.

"You never have to be perfect for me," I told her as I wrapped my arms around her waist. "Just being you is more than enough."

She laid her head on my shoulder and sighed contentedly. "You'll probably never know how much I value that," she whispered. "I feel the same way about you."

I knew she did.

She liked me just as much as I liked her, even though I'd made some mistakes.

It was a little addictive to be liked for the man I was and not because I was Kaleb Remington.

She'd probably never know how much that meant to me, either.

"Should I make us something to eat?" she finally asked.

I tightened my arms around her waist. "I'll help you in a few minutes."

Strangely, I wanted to savor the moment and my connection with this incredible woman just a little while longer.

# Chapter 6

*Anna*

I closed the book I was reading two days later, stretched, and then glanced at the clock.

It was late. I'd gotten absorbed in my reading material and had completely lost track of the time.

I felt good, much better than I had for a long time.

Appparently, the peace and isolation of this cabin and Kaleb's company was therapeutic for me.

Sometimes Kaleb and I talked a lot.

Sometimes we just read in silence, but those quiet times were never uncomfortable.

Oddly, I was never bored, even though I was always busy in my normal life.

I was enjoying the peace of being away from the world and the constant work pressures for a little while.

Being here with Kaleb just felt...right.

Unfortunately for me, I was wildly attracted to him physically, but I'd managed to tamp down the carnal urge to rip his clothes off so far. But the more I got to know him, the more I craved that kind of intimacy with him.

*Dial it back, Anna. That absolutely cannot happen.*

Having sex with a man who made me feel safe would be totally insane, but that didn't stop me from wanting that more than I'd wanted anything for a very long time.

Instinctively, I knew he was the one man who could completely rock my world, but Kaleb was off-limits. Never once had he given me any sign that he wanted anything more than the connection we had right now.

*Don't get too attached. That connection will be broken soon.*

The storm had passed, and we were just waiting for the massive amount of snow to be cleared from the roads, which would likely happen tomorrow.

It wasn't like I hadn't known that the time I got to spend with Kaleb was severely limited, but it hurt to know that we'd be parting ways soon.

The man wasn't a stranger anymore, and he'd helped me more than I ever thought possible in just a few days.

We'd healed each other a little by using each other as a sounding board.

Neither of us had definitive answers for the other, but just trying to reason things out together had been helpful. At least it had been for me.

I'd found temporary solace with him, and I dreaded the moment when I'd have to let that go.

I glanced at Kaleb, who was just putting his book away on the other side of the couch, a western paperback that had belonged to his father.

"Your mother has an eclectic collection of books," I told Kaleb.

"Are you complaining?" he questioned. "You've devoured enough of her reading material."

"Not at all. I have the same type of library. I think I'd probably like her."

"I'm positive you'd adore her," Kaleb answered. "You two have a lot in common, and she speaks her mind just like you do."

I nodded. "Then I'd definitely like her. We even have the same taste in art. I'm actually jealous that she owns so many original paintings by M. Remington. I only have one, and I treasure that painting. Does she know her? I think the artist still lives here in Montana."

I'd been surprised once I'd gotten close enough to the landscapes on the walls to notice the distinct style and unmistakable signature in the corner.

M. Remington was probably the best known, living, contemporary western landscape artist in the country. Still, it wasn't easy to lay hands on one of her original paintings, much less a cabin full of them.

I put my book on the side table.

*Silence.*

I glanced at Kaleb, and for once, he looked like he had no idea what to say.

"Are you okay?" I asked, concerned.

It wasn't like Kaleb to not say what he was thinking. Once we'd gotten through the getting-to-know-you part of our relationship, he'd been pretty open with me about most things.

He glanced at me and our gazes locked.

"I'm good," he said in a serious tone. "I'm just not sure how to answer that question without lying, and I refuse to lie to you, Anna."

"Then she does know her," I said excitedly.

"I know her, too," Kaleb said flatly.

My eyes widened. "You don't have to tell me if you don't want to, but I swear I'll never tell anyone about anything you say right now."

He shook his head. "It isn't that I don't trust you with anything we want to discuss. Hell, I've spilled my guts to you about things I don't talk about with anyone. However, if I tell you, it would reveal more than we agreed to share."

I was immediately contrite. "I'm sorry. I didn't know."

We had made a pact to just be Kaleb and Anna without revealing anything we didn't want to talk about.

Personally, I didn't give a damn about our original agreement anymore. I trusted Kaleb.

In fact, I *wanted* to tell Kaleb everything, and I planned on doing just that before we parted ways.

I didn't want him to discover the truth someday and think that I'd played him for a fool.

Maybe it had only been a few days, but he'd come to mean too much to me not to be totally honest.

"I have no problem crossing that line, Anna," he said in a husky voice, his gorgeous eyes glued to mine. "Not if you don't. Are you really ready to go back to Los Angeles? If you're not, I'd like you to come back to Crystal Fork with me. Take as long as you want to grieve and heal before you head back to California. No pressure, but I have plenty of space at my place, and I'd really like it if you'd come home with me."

My breath left my body in an audible *whoosh!*

He had no idea how tempted I was to take him up on that offer.

I'd only rented the home down the road for a few days. Just enough time to get my head together a little.

I was more together, but was I ready to go back to California and jump into my old life immediately?

Honestly, I wasn't.

I felt like I was ready to do some work, but not to fall back into the life I'd lived before.

Not yet.

I wasn't as strong as I needed to be for my lifestyle, and I was afraid that the pressures I had to face in Los Angeles would crush the progress I'd made so far.

Kaleb's invitation was sincere. He actually did want me to go with him. I could see it in his eyes, and I'd learned enough about Kaleb to know that he wasn't a guy who offered to do something just to be polite.

God, I really, really wanted to accept that invitation.

"I'd really like that, but it could get…complicated."

He still knew next to nothing about my life in California.

He smiled ruefully. "I always thought I didn't do complicated, but you're definitely an exception to that rule. I don't really give a shit if this complicates the hell out of my life, Anna. All I know right now is that I'm not even remotely ready to say goodbye to you. I also think you need more time before you throw yourself back into your old life. It sounds like more stress than you need right now."

Like it or not, Kaleb had assigned himself the job of being my older, male protector.

While there was a part of me that loved that alpha protector side of him, there was also a big piece of me that wanted him to see me as more than just a friend and a female who he needed to protect.

I wanted him to look at me like I was a woman he desired because I knew I looked at him like a man I definitely wanted to know intimately.

Was I hiding it well?

*Probably.*

I was a master at hiding my emotions when other people were around me.

However, I wondered just how long it would be before he realized that I desperately wanted to go to bed with him and do more than just sleep in the same bed or use his body heat as my personal electric blanket.

Probably the last thing I needed was an intimate relationship to mess with my head right now, but I wouldn't really have to worry about that since Kaleb wasn't attracted to me that way.

I definitely wanted to spend more time with him, but did I dare? And would he still even want me to come with him once he realized the truth about my identity?

"It would definitely be complicated," I warned him again.

"How complicated can it be?" he asked, his tone unconcerned.

Oh, hell, he had no idea.

"So are you going to tell me how you know M. Remington?" I asked curiously.

I was going to tell Kaleb everything shortly, but I was dying to know how he was connected to my favorite artist.

"What do you know about her?" he questioned.

"Not much, unfortunately," I told him. "She's pretty private, so there isn't a lot of personal details out there about her life. I did read somewhere a long time ago that she was married to a rancher here in Montana, and I think that very brief bio said that she has three insanely rich sons."

"She does," he acknowledged.

"So tell me how you know her," I insisted. "Does she live somewhere near Crystal Fork?"

"She lives *in* Crystal Fork," he corrected. "What you read was correct. She still lives on that ranch outside of town."

"So you probably know her well," I said with a sigh.

"I know her very well. Millie Remington is my mother, Anna, and I'm one of those insanely rich sons."

## Chapter 7

*Kaleb*

I wasn't certain whether the shock on her face was a good thing or a bad thing.

Hell, maybe that hadn't been the right way to tell her that Millie Remington was my mother, but I thought it might be better if I just got it over with and done.

If she was going to come to Crystal Fork with me, she'd have to know the truth, and I was done with being anonymous. I needed her to trust me completely so she'd come back to Crystal Fork with me.

I wanted her to know everything now. We'd reached the point where it was hard to keep dancing around the details of our lives.

Yeah, I knew we could never be anything but friends, but I still wanted to be there for her. I'd come to value that friendship and our connection, and her well-being was more important than my desire to fuck her senseless.

Anna was far from being a helpless woman, but she was in a period of her life when she needed someone she could trust in a relaxed environment.

Maybe after she'd worked through her grief and confusion, I'd feel a lot less uneasy about watching her go back to Los Angeles.

I'd feel like I was throwing her to the wolves if she went back to California alone at the moment.

She wasn't ready.

She might talk like she had it all together most of the time, but she didn't need to be alone in a big city with a ton of pressure on her. Not when she could stay with me until she was ready.

"What?" she finally squeaked. "She's…your mother?"

I wasn't sure whether I was glad or insulted that she'd never even given my insanely rich status a second thought. She seemed much more impressed I was related to M. Remington.

I nodded. "My full name is Kaleb Remington. My brothers and I own a company called KTD Remington. It's the largest privately owned holding company in America."

She raised an eyebrow teasingly. "So, I guess that makes you kind of a big deal, huh?"

I chuckled. "Some people think so."

"Do women throw themselves at you on a daily basis because you're uber rich and hot?"

*Shit!* How was I supposed to answer *that*? "Not on a daily basis, no. My brothers and I keep pretty low profiles. We live in the small town we grew up in, and our headquarters in Billings doesn't have a lot of staff turnover. Most of our employees have been there for years. My life is pretty uneventful the majority of the time."

"I think you're full of crap, Kaleb Remington," she said with a delighted laugh. "Or you're looking for a way not to admit that women fall all over you. It's not like there are a lot of gorgeous, single billionaires in Montana."

"I don't really date," I grumbled. "The women that I've dated in the past were more interested in my money than they ever were in me."

She frowned at me. "I doubt that's true. The money and your hotness might initially attract a lot of women, but I can't imagine that any sane woman wouldn't be interested in you once they get to know you. I can honestly say I don't give a damn about your money or that you're some kind of business tycoon. I care about *you*."

*Fuck!* I knew that. It was probably one of the reasons I couldn't let her go.

Anna had liked me even when she thought I was a furniture maker. In my world, that was a pretty rare gift.

I swallowed the lump in my throat and simply answered, "I care about you, too. That's why I want you to come to Crystal Fork with me. You need more time, Anna, and it's a friendly little town most of the time."

She chewed on her lower lip as she glanced at me.

Unfortunately, I could still see her hesitation, and it made my gut hurt.

What in the hell was making her so wary? Not once had I seen real fear in her eyes, even when she'd woken up half naked and on my lap in the very beginning.

"I suppose it's my turn to tell you who I really am," she said with a long sigh. "You might change your mind about that invitation. Like I said, my life is really complicated, and if I come with you, you might get more attention than you want to get."

"Who you really are isn't going to matter to me, Anna. You already assured me that you're not a criminal and that you're not being chased by a crazy stalker. I can handle whatever you tell me."

She shifted until she was sitting on the edge of the couch.

Anna reached for her phone and pulled up her photos.

She took a deep breath as she brought up a picture. "I was grateful that you didn't recognize me when I fell through your window, and I'll always be glad that you got to know me as just Anna. But there's a big part of my life that you don't know, Kaleb."

She handed me her phone without saying another word.

My eyes shifted to the photo, and my jaw dropped as I perused it closely for a few moments.

I didn't realize that it was Anna in that photo until I carefully compared the facial features, but I *had* immediately recognized the name on the album cover.

I looked at her and back at the picture again, my brain in total denial, even though I logically knew that the woman in the picture and my Anna were one and the same. The distinctive eyes were a dead giveaway.

Now that I knew her, I'd always be able to recognize those unique eyes of hers.

"Christ! Is it true? Are you really Annelise?" I asked hoarsely as our eyes met.

Other than those unforgettable eyes, nothing in the photo looked like Anna.

The image had a woman in heavy makeup and thick, very long blonde hair. The album cover looked slightly familiar, but since I didn't follow the pop music culture, I'd probably never paid that much attention to it in the past.

She nodded slowly as she looked at me like she was afraid of my reaction. "My full name is Annelise Kendrick, but people who know me call me Anna."

Okay, this definitely wasn't the reveal that I was expecting.

In fact, I was having a hard time processing her real identity.

Anna was one of the hottest pop artists in the world, and had been for many years. She was so well known that people rarely used her last name anymore. She was simply known as Annelise.

I suddenly felt a little idiotic for not recognizing her.

I shook my head. "I didn't recognize you. I don't follow the pop scene. I know your name. Everyone does. I've seen you perform briefly, but I didn't connect you with Annelise."

"I'm glad that you didn't," she said softly. "Before I left, my friend, Kim, tried to alter my appearance as much as possible. She dyed my hair back to its natural color and cut it all off. My hair has always been my most recognizable feature. I look a lot more normal without it. But even though I look different, I'm still worried that if I go into a populated place, someone will still recognize me."

I handed her phone back to her. "They might," I conceded, finally getting used to the idea that Annelise and my Anna were the same woman. "Especially if they're a huge fan. But it's entirely possible that you won't be recognized. If someone thinks they know who you are, you can always blow them off and tell them you get that all the time. You can acknowledge that you sort of have the same features, but laugh it off and tell them you're not Annelise. I live outside of town. No one will bother you on my property."

"If someone recognizes me, the press will be all over that within hours if they get wind of my location and who I'm staying with in Montana. For the most part, no one bothers me much in Los Angeles. The locals are used to seeing celebrities everywhere. But it would be a juicy story if I was shacked up with a very eligible billionaire in Montana. The press would want to know who you are and if there's a romantic relationship between the two of us. That would be hell for you," she murmured fearfully.

I shrugged. "Do I look worried? I have property, Anna. It's not like they're going to be allowed to camp out on my front lawn. Tell me the whole story about what happened to you that made you leave California."

I reached out, snagged her body and tugged her next to me because she looked terrified.

Anna wasn't worried that the press would find her. It probably happened to her all the time when she wasn't in Los Angeles. She was actually concerned about inconveniencing…me.

She slowly relaxed against me. "I found out that my parents were murdered right before the last concert on my mega tour, which was in Los Angeles. I'm not sure how I got through that night. I think a large part of me was functioning on autopilot, Kaleb. Right after it ended, I went to my dressing room, and I had no idea what to do. My brain shut down to the point where I barely knew my own name. All I could think about was escaping to get my head on straight again. The press would have had a field day if they'd seen that meltdown. Kim came and picked me up, and I stayed at her place for the night. Both of us have become experts at evading the press when I don't want to be interviewed, and they will chase me down if I give them something to write about. We went to her shop the next day after it closed, and she did my transformation. I hired a private charter service to fly here, and I was in Montana by the following morning. You pretty much know the rest. I missed the driveway I was supposed to go down and ended up here in the middle of a blizzard."

I thought about all of the things she'd told me without telling me she was a famous pop music icon.

Her weird hours.

Foregoing her college degree for a lucrative opportunity.

Being a workaholic.

The constant stress of her career, which I'd actually highly underestimated.

Needing to get away from Los Angeles because she wasn't functioning well.

All of those details about her life suddenly fell into place and made sense to me.

She'd been famous for a long time, but I couldn't remember a single scandal that was attached to her.

She obviously was a workaholic without a real personal life.

I'd gotten to know her, and I was certain that she wasn't into the Hollywood party scene.

She'd actually teased me about women falling over *me*. Hell, she could have any guy she wanted with a crook of her finger. She wasn't just beautiful and kind. Anna was incredibly famous.

"Everything I've ever told you is true," she murmured quietly. "I just left out some of the details. I planned on telling you the truth before we parted ways."

"I don't blame you for not sharing the truth with a stranger. We both agreed not to talk about some of the details of our lives. So music was your opportunity? The reason you decided against your college plans?"

"Actually, I'd already been accepted to Juilliard," she explained thoughtfully. "I loved pop music, but I didn't grow up dying to be famous. My original plan was to be a concert pianist. I was gifted on the piano, and my parents worked their butts off to keep me in classical lessons from the time I was five years old. I was discovered by a record producer who was on vacation in Bozeman. I was messing

## Chapter 8

*Anna*

"Your place is enormous," I informed Kaleb the next day as we sat in his gigantic kitchen in Crystal Fork. "I almost got lost coming back downstairs. But it's beautiful here. I understand why you never want to leave."

The plows had cleared the main roads near the cabin early this morning, and the caretaker had plowed the ridiculously long driveway. Soon after the snow had been cleared, he'd arranged to have my rental car returned, and his helicopter had arrived to take us to Crystal Fork.

The man had a private helicopter, a private jet, and he and his brothers had built their own private airport close to their properties to handle their arrivals and departures.

I'd discovered that when Kaleb Remington wanted something, he got it almost instantly.

I'd understood that he was rich and powerful, but seeing that wealth and power in action was a little overwhelming.

When he gave a command…things just magically happened without question.

Helicopters arrived.

Rental cars got returned.

Driveways got cleared.

People jumped to do Kaleb's bidding. Probably because that was what they were paid to do.

It was like two different men dwelled in his gorgeous body. The bossy billionaire that people jumped to serve and the kind but gruff guy I'd gotten to know at the cabin.

He'd even managed to provide me with the same coffee maker that was at the cabin with the same supplies before we'd even arrived in Crystal Fork.

Maybe he was a little bossy and abrupt in his public life, but he was still the same Kaleb that I'd come to adore when we were alone.

He shrugged nonchalantly. "I lived in New York for a while after college. I worked on Wall Street. My brothers joined me there after they finished college. I was happy when our business took off fairly quickly and I was able to relocate back to Montana. I like my space. Was your room okay?"

*Okay?*

Yeah, it was definitely okay.

It was significantly more decadent than the suites I stayed in when I was on tour, and probably even bigger than those temporary accommodations.

I owned a very nice house in Beverly Hills, but it was nothing like this over the top mansion.

"My suite is gorgeous," I told him after I took a sip of the coffee I'd just made. "Your decorator has good taste. I saw the barn outside. It's enormous. You must have a lot of horses."

Most of his home was modern and professionally decorated, but it was still warm with some western touches. His living room was filled with his mother's paintings, each one different, but with the same, unique, M. Remington style.

I hadn't found the music room yet, but I had time to search it out later.

"I have several of them," he confirmed. "Do you ride?"

"I haven't for a long time, unfortunately," I said wistfully. "We didn't have the money for horses when I was a kid, but a lot of my neighbors had them. I rode as often as I could."

"I've got the perfect horse for you if you feel like riding. She's a little too small for me, but she'd be perfect for you," Kaleb informed me.

I smiled at him. "I'd love that, but I can wait until tomorrow. I'd love to explore this house and take a walk around your property later."

It would probably take me a while to get my bearings in a house this big, and I was dying to get outside after being cooped up in the cabin for days.

Temperatures had risen considerably, and this area hadn't gotten that much snow from the storm we'd ridden out at the cabin.

"I might have to go into the office tomorrow to wrap some things up," he warned.

"I'll be fine here alone," I assured him. "I'm pretty good at adapting to a new location, and I need to work a little, too."

My cell phone started to ring, and I silenced it immediately. "My agent," I explained. "He's livid that I didn't tell him where I was and what I was doing. He's been badgering Kim to tell him where I am. I'll call him later."

"He's not your damn keeper," Kaleb rumbled irritably.

I snorted. "He thinks he is. He wants me to confirm another tour next year, and I probably should. I've never had a year without a big tour, but my head just isn't there right now. Performing in front of huge crowds has always stressed me out. I have terrible stage fright."

He shot me a doubtful look. "How is that possible after all these years? If you started in entertainment after high school, it's been what? Seventeen years?"

I nodded. "It's part of my job," I explained. "But it's not my favorite part. Don't get me wrong, I love and appreciate all of my fans, but I'd rather write and record music than get out on a stage in front of a huge crowd. It's always been that way for me. I'm usually terrified before a performance, even after all these years of doing it. That fear has never really gone away. I've just learned to hide that fear and push through it better."

"Why don't you stop doing the big tours if you don't like that part of it?" he asked.

I shook my head. "It's not that simple. A large chunk of my income is made with my tours. Royalties and record deals don't pay as well as touring. Ray, my agent, drills that into my head almost every day. If I could quit the big tours, I'd do it, at least for a little while. I've lived out of a suitcase for my entire adult life. It would be nice to take a break."

"Anna, you must have made a fortune. You've been a pop icon for a long time. If your money is invested well, you could quit doing those mega tours right now. Write music. Record that music. Do appearances where you want, when you want. Do what makes *you* happy."

God, I really wished that was possible. I'd felt like a puppet on strings for so long that I wasn't really sure how to do exactly what I wanted.

I swallowed a sip of coffee before I answered. "You're probably going to think this is crazy, but my dad handled a lot of my investing and my business finances. He was good at it. Financial management isn't one of my strong points, and I'm always so busy that I almost never have a chance to sit down and try to understand it more. Ray says I need to tour, so I tour."

Kaleb shot me a troubled frown. "Your agent is handling all of your business finances now?"

"Ray was my dad's friend," I told him. "Or maybe you could say that my dad was like a substitute father to him. I've known Ray since I was a kid. He lived next door. When his own father died, my dad took him under his wing. He's been helping me since the beginning of my career. He handles a few other artists now, but he got his start by handling my gigs for me. I didn't have an agent in the beginning. My father was good with financial stuff, and I was eighteen."

Kaleb nodded distractedly. "I get that, but didn't you ever think about getting a financial manager once you started making more money?"

"Dad always consulted me on the things he was doing, and he liked handling my financial stuff," I mused. "After he died, Ray said he had it handled. I know I need to find someone, but I haven't started looking for someone yet. Honestly, I'm not sure where to start or who to hire."

"You trust Ray," Kaleb stated, his expression still somewhat concerned. "I understand that he's a personal friend, too, but I wouldn't mind taking a look at your portfolio just to make sure your gains are being optimized. Maybe I can help reassure you that you can stop doing big tours if it doesn't make you happy. It never hurts to have more than one set of eyes on a portfolio. Finance and investments are my specialties."

I shot him a grateful look. "If you wouldn't mind, I'd happily accept that offer. I have a ballpark figure of how much money I have invested, and my dad used to be meticulous about my financial records. I never really had to dig into those investments, and I never seemed to have the time. I do trust Ray, but I haven't figured out what I'm going to do about all of the things my dad used to handle for me yet. Now that he's gone, I know I need an expert working with my money and investments. I have the latest portfolio and records that Dad sent to me right before he died."

"Perfect," Kaleb said. "Send them to me and I'll look things over for you."

"I feel like an of idiot that I don't handle my own financial—"

"Don't," Kaleb interrupted firmly. "Most people in your position don't handle the everyday business stuff or investments. It's complicated for people in your field. That's why wealth managers and business managers have a job. You're incredibly creative, Anna. You have an enormous amount of responsibilities on you. Don't beat yourself up because you don't have the time or the energy to be an investment and financial expert, too."

That made me feel a little better. "I always hated math in school," I confessed sheepishly.

"Yeah, well," he grumbled. "If it makes you feel better, you have more artistic talent than most people could ever dream of having. I certainly don't have that. My mother is a renowned artist, and I can't even draw. Tanner inherited her talent, and Devon is musical, but I'm not exactly a creative guy."

"You make some incredible furniture," I reminded him.

"That's all I can create," he said in a self-mocking voice.

I laughed because he looked so disgruntled. The man was a billionaire and a business tycoon. *That* was his special talent.

It would be completely unfair if he was good at *everything*.

He was hot.

He was rich.

He was a business genius.

He was thoughtful and generous.

In my mind, he didn't need to have artistic talent, too.

"Will I get to meet your mom and your brothers before I leave?"

Kaleb smirked. "Do you honestly think I'll have a choice in whether you meet them or not? My brothers have a very bad habit of dropping in whenever they feel like it, so I'll have to tell them I have a guest. If my brothers know you're here, my mother will eventually find out. I'm not saying my family is intrusive, but they make themselves at home here if I let them. Mom won't be able to contain her curiosity. Especially if she knows I have a female guest. She doesn't complain too much, but she makes it perfectly clear that she wants us married and having her grandchildren. She finally gave up on trying to set us up with nice women, but she's still hopeful. Mom will find some way of finagling her way into the house. Knowing her, she'll thaw out some of the huckleberries she has in the freezer and make a pie to bribe her way in."

Kaleb's annoyed comments didn't match the look in his eyes.

He obviously adored his family, even if they did invade his space sometimes.

"Oh, God," I groaned as I rubbed my belly. "I love huckleberry pie. It's been a long time since I've had some. I'm afraid that kind of bribery would definitely work on me."

Montana had the most amazing wild huckleberries, a berry that didn't grow in that many states. Thinking back on it, I probably hadn't had a huckleberry since I'd left Montana seventeen years ago.

*Billionaire Unexplained*

"Fair warning," Kaleb said drily. "My mother makes the best huckleberry pie in Montana, and she's not ashamed of using that to her advantage to get what she wants."

I laughed. "I'm sure that your family is just as amazing as you are. I can't wait to meet them all."

"Yo! Kaleb!" a loud baritone bellowed from the living room.

"Shit!" Kaleb cursed. "They probably heard the helicopter."

"You here?" another low, male voice inquired insistently. "It's about time you got your ass back home."

"My brothers," he said, sounding resigned. "Unfortunately, they have a key that I'm going to have to confiscate immediately."

I smiled. "It's okay. I wish I was a little better dressed to meet your family, but I'm excited to meet them. I'm curious to see if they're as handsome as you are."

"They aren't," he grumbled.

I stood and smoothed down my hair.

I was in a ratty pair of jeans that had seen better days, and a red T-shirt that had shrunk one too many times in the dryer.

When I was home, it was the way I always dressed. And I'd planned on being alone in the wilderness. Almost every clothing item I had with me was comfortable, staying-at-home clothes with the exception of one casual dress that I'd thrown into my suitcase at the last minute. I wasn't used to leaving home without something I could wear in public if needed.

Kaleb stood and grabbed my hand that was messing with my hair. "Don't fuss. You look beautiful, and they're idiots."

Two very large men came into the kitchen bickering back and forth about something that was incomprehensible.

I had my answer to my question about whether or not they were as handsome as Kaleb almost immediately.

Maybe they weren't quite as handsome as Kaleb, but they were still ridiculously gorgeous.

One of them had beautiful, black hair, and the other sported a shade of brown that was a little darker than Kaleb's.

God, it really should be impossible for three brothers in one family to all be this good-looking.

Both of them halted and immediately stopped griping to each other as they saw Kaleb and me standing in the kitchen.

The silence in the room was a little unnerving as they surveyed me and tried to figure out what was going on.

Obviously, Kaleb didn't have female visitors often because they looked...perplexed.

The brother with black hair finally stepped forward, tilted his head, and stared to the point of rudeness before he finally spoke. "We didn't know that you had company, bro. How in the hell did you meet Annelise, and why is she here in Crystal Fork?"

## Chapter 9

*Kaleb*

*Fuck!* I probably should have anticipated that Devon would immediately recognize Annelise.

He was the musician in the family, and he loved almost all types of music. Most likely, he'd seen all of her music videos a million times.

He also never forgot a face.

It had taken him a moment, but he'd figured out her identity fairly quickly.

On the other hand, Tanner still looked confused.

Probably because, like me, he wasn't that into the pop charts or the music scene.

"Anna," I said as I silently cursed Devon for not taking his eyes off her. "These are my brothers, Tanner and Devon." I pointed to each one of them as I said their names so there was no confusion about who was who.

Devon, my youngest brother, had jet black hair, so she was unlikely to confuse the two in the future.

She stepped forward and offered her hand. "It's nice to meet both of you. I'm Annelise Kendrick, but I'd really like it if you'd call me Anna."

One big smile from Anna, and she had my brothers eating out of her hand.

Tanner grinned back at her and shook her hand.

Devon gave her one of his charming smiles that only showed up when he was trying to get someone to do what he wanted them to do. Or...when he found a woman extremely attractive.

*The little bastard!*

He really needed to back off.

Even though Anna and I weren't a couple, there was no way I could watch my youngest brother try to charm her out of her panties.

*Not. Happening.*

"I didn't recognize you until Devon said something," Tanner said remorsefully. "You look different..."

Tanner's voice trailed off, probably because he didn't know what to say without sounding rude.

"Without all that blonde hair," Devon chimed in. "Why exactly did you say you were in Crystal Fork?"

"She didn't, and it's none of your business," I growled. "Anna is my guest. She's here to get some rest and relaxation. Don't tell anyone that she's here."

"I've heard some rumors that she's gone MIA from Los Angeles," Devon mused.

"How did you hear that?" Anna asked with a startled look on her face.

I shot my youngest brother an annoyed look.

"What?" he said in a pseudo innocent tone. "One of our subsidiaries is a record label. I have friends there. I hear things sometimes. I think her agent has been frantically searching for her."

The recording company was Devon's project pick, so he did handle most of the necessary business for that company. He liked keeping up on what was happening in the music scene.

"So now everyone knows I left the city without telling anyone?" Anna asked with a resigned sigh.

"Probably not everybody," Devon said, probably backpedaling because Anna looked so forlorn. "But he's been finding people you know to see if they know where you are."

"Fuck!" I cursed. "You'd think that an agent who is also supposed to be a friend would give her some damn space and keep his mouth shut."

Anna was his client. He should be discreet and not be causing any speculation for her sake. She had called him. Her agent knew she wasn't in danger. She didn't have any appearances scheduled right now. Why in the hell was he so determined to find her?

"Why?" Devon asked. "Why did you change your appearance and leave? Are you in trouble with the law or something?"

"Devon," Tanner said in a warning voice. "Leave it alone."

My middle brother was always the voice of reason.

I was the hothead sometimes.

And Devon was the irritating little brother without a filter.

"No," Anna said as she shook her head.

"Anna," I said firmly, trying to let her know that she didn't owe anyone an explanation.

She held up a hand. "It's okay. They're your brothers. I have no problem sharing some of why I'm here."

I listened irritably as she shared what she wanted my brothers to know.

Like how she tried to break into the cabin to avoid freezing to death.

Her parents' deaths six months ago.

Her need to get away for a while and not have to deal with the press.

Her exhaustion from a recent music tour.

She was even open about her grief, but she left out the part about her mental meltdown after her last concert. Probably because she was still confused about that episode herself.

Personally, I didn't find that meltdown strange at all considering how much she'd had on her plate at the time and the grief she was going through.

However, I wasn't surprised that she didn't want to share that kind of vulnerability with two men she didn't know.

"God, Anna, I'm so sorry," Tanner said in a genuine tone. "We were all broken after we lost our father. I can't imagine losing both of my parents at the same time. Somebody needs to shut your agent down. You could use some peace and privacy after what happened."

"I didn't take much time off after my parents died," she explained. "Work was really all I had left. I have no other close family. I think I'm just mentally drained."

"We'll keep your secret," Devon vowed.

"Mom is going to find out," Tanner added. "But she knows how to keep a secret."

"I'm excited to meet her," Anna said enthusiastically. "I'm a huge fan of her art."

"The first thing she's going to ask is if you and Kaleb are dating," Tanner warned.

"Are you?" Devon asked.

"No, we aren't," I snapped. "Anna is a...friend. She's an international pop star. Do you honestly think the two of us would be dating?"

Devon shook his head slowly. "You're a billionaire, and it's not like you're that much older than her. It was an obvious assumption."

"The last thing she needs is a relationship with *anyone*," I rumbled, hoping that Devon got the message not to mess with Anna. "She's here to relax. After I wrap some things up at the office tomorrow, I'm taking some time off to do the same."

Tanner's head jerked abruptly in my direction, his expression shocked. "Seriously? You're actually going to take some kind of vacation?"

"I know it's been a while—"

"A while?" Devon interrupted. "You *never* take any time off for yourself."

"I'm trying to change that," I replied defensively.

"About time," Tanner said. "What can we do to try to keep Anna's presence a secret?"

"Do you know where I can get a pair of fake glasses?" Anna asked jokingly.

"I can wrangle some up if you need them. Are you going to try to go into town?" Tanner asked.

"I'm not sure," Anna answered. "I'd love to see Crystal Fork, but I don't want to bring the press here. That would be miserable for everyone."

"We'll decide later," I told Tanner. "Let's see how things go."

"You do realize that the town's spring fundraiser is Sunday, right?" Devon questioned. "Mom is in charge of it this year, and we all volunteered to help."

"Fuck!" I cursed, irritated. "I did forget. We donate a small fortune to the town every year. I don't know why they still have to do the fundraiser."

"What is it?" Anna asked curiously.

"It's a yearly event," Tanner explained. "And they still do it because it's a tradition. It's not really about the money anymore. People love the baked goods, the food, the things for sale, and the auction. It's more of a social event for the whole town than a fundraiser. The proceeds go to our small library, the fire department, and the police department."

"That sounds amazing," Anna said excitedly.

"Maybe the event will get rained out," I said hopefully.

Generally, I liked helping with the spring fundraiser. The town did love the event, and my whole family had been pitching in to help as long as I could remember. But I really didn't want to take off for the day so soon after her arrival and leave Anna kicking around on her own until after dinner.

I'd figure something out.

There were a lot of people there to help, and my mother would understand if I couldn't make it this year.

"I've gotten pretty good at disguising myself so I can go out in public when I'm not in Los Angeles," Anna pondered. "It's a few days away. Maybe I could help, too. I'd like that. It's been so long since I've attended a community event."

The longing in her beautiful eyes made me want to take her anywhere she wanted to go.

Her profession came with so many personal restrictions that prohibited her from living a normal life, and I hated that for her.

Would people recognize her here in Crystal Fork?

Tanner and I hadn't, but there were bound to be people here like Devon who would recognize those distinctive eyes of hers.

Anyone who had looked at a closeup photo or video of hers would probably recognize those dark, expressive eyes.

Yeah, her eyes were brown, which was the most common color of eyes, but Anna's were a deep, dark chocolate color with tiny, lighter flecks the color of honey that made them especially unforgettable.

"We could get her some colored contact lenses," Devon said thoughtfully.

"Maybe some sunglasses," Tanner suggested.

"I have both," Anna informed us. "I haven't tried the blue contacts yet, but my eye doctor prescribed them for me right before I left California. I tossed them in my purse, so I do have them with me. Do you think that would help?"

"Yes," all of us said in unison.

Apparently I wasn't the only one who had noticed that very distinctive feature of hers.

"She's also going to need a backstory," Devon pointed out. "Why she's here. A different occupation. I don't think people would question her presence here as much if she was here for a different and plausible reason.'

I still wasn't sure that Anna should expose herself to the public. It was risky, and when it came to her, I was extremely risk-averse.

But it was almost impossible for me to deny her when she turned her yearning gaze toward me.

"I just want to be normal for a little while," she pleaded.

*Fuck!* How was I supposed to protest when she wanted that so damn much?

"I honestly think we can pull this off," Tanner said in a low, cautious voice. "But Devon is right. She needs a good backstory."

"It's not like she can be an old college friend," I said drily. "She'd never pass for being my age."

Anna looked way younger than thirty-five.

"Since everyone knows all you ever do is work, it would be better if this was a friendly work relationship of some kind," Devon contemplated.

"Marketing," Anna decided. "At least it's an occupation I know something about."

"Perfect," Tanner agreed. "We could tell everyone she's here from California to help you overhaul a new company brand."

"We have our own people for that," I balked.

"Nobody knows that," Tanner pointed out. "Tell people that she's a friend, a marketing specialist that's here to work with you on a project."

"I could make people believe that," Anna said confidently. "I've become an expert at promoting my own brand."

I nodded slowly. It was probably the only thing that made sense, especially if Anna would be comfortable in that role. "I still don't like taking this risk, but it's probably the best story we can use."

"Mom is going to have to be in on all this," Devon mentioned. "We suck at lying to her. She always knows when we're full of shit."

"I wouldn't want you to lie to your mother for me anyway," Anna said adamantly. "I'll tell her the truth."

We talked a little longer about the specifics of Anna's new identity, and then my brothers said they needed to leave.

"I'll walk you out," I told Devon and Tanner as we headed for the front door.

Anna waved at my brothers and thanked them profusely for helping her, but stayed behind in the kitchen.

As soon as we hit the living room, Tanner mumbled in a low voice, "Nobody is going to believe that you're not attracted to her as something other than a friend."

"Agreed," Devon added. "You look at her like you can't wait to get her naked, and you have to tone down that protective instinct. You said that you aren't dating, but I've never seen you look at a woman like you'd rip the head off anyone who touches her."

I looked at Tanner for verification.

"He's right," Tanner confirmed, and then released a long breath. "Maybe we only notice it because we're family, but you need to loosen up, brother. Otherwise, you'll never be able to convince people that you're just friends and colleagues."

I wasn't going to bullshit my brothers. It would never work. We were way too tight. "I can't help it. She's been through a lot. I want to help her, and I feel like someone should protect her. No one else has stepped up to the plate for her."

"It's more than that," Devon said. "You're attracted to her. Not that I blame you. Are you sure there isn't more to this story than you're telling us right now? You were with Annelise in a remote cabin. That's a lot of temptation for a guy to handle. She's also really nice."

"No, there's nothing more," I said tightly. "Everything she told you is true, and she's not interested in me that way."

"Unrequited lust must really suck. Not that I've ever experienced it myself," Devon said jokingly.

Tanner smacked Devon on the back of his head. "Don't be an asshole, Devon." Then he turned to me. "You okay with all of this?"

I shrugged. "I have to be. The alternative is letting her go back to California when she really needs to escape for a while, and that's not an option for me."

"I get it," Tanner said as he pushed Devon out the front door. "She's an easy woman to like, but I'm not totally convinced the attraction isn't mutual."

"I am," I muttered. Anna had never given me a single reason to think that she wanted more than a friendship. "If you talk to Mom, tell her I'll stop by tomorrow night."

Tanner nodded and left after shooting me an unsettled glance.

I closed the door behind him and headed back toward the kitchen.

My brothers both liked Anna, but I knew that Tanner was concerned that I might be getting in over my head with this situation.

Hell, maybe he was right, but I'd happily dive off the deep end if necessary if it meant that Anna was safe and happy.

# Chapter 10

*Anna*

"It's beautiful here," I told Kaleb with a happy sigh the following afternoon.

We'd ridden Kaleb's horses to the small river that ran through his property, where we'd dismounted to admire the views.

As promised, he'd hooked me up with the perfect horse, an Arabian bay colored mare that he called Bella because her registered name was much too complicated. It had been a long time since I'd been on a horse, but she was so well-mannered and sweet that it really didn't matter.

It was late afternoon, and the scene in front of us was like something out of one of his mother's paintings.

We had a perfect view of the mountains, and the stream was swelled and running swiftly from the snow melt.

The weather had changed completely, and it now felt like spring in Montana. I'd brought my jacket, but I hadn't needed it with the sweatshirt and jeans that I was currently wearing.

Kaleb had gone to Billings earlier in the day to finish some work, and I'd scoped out his incredible house, starting with the music room on the main floor.

It was equipped with a grand piano that was a joy to play, several guitars, and multiple other musical instruments that he likely didn't play. It was decorated in soothing colors that had made me relax enough to do a little writing.

Kaleb had been home by early afternoon, still dressed in a custom suit that had taken my breath away.

After spending time with him in nothing but casual clothing, his business look was a little startling, but definitely not unattractive.

He was a man of many personas, and I adored all of them.

They were all Kaleb, and unfortunately for me, all of those different personalities were compelling.

The man was drop-dead gorgeous, whether he was casually dressed for the wilderness or in a custom suit.

Some people might say that he was ruggedly handsome, which was apparently an aphrodisiac for me.

I was constantly surrounded by good looking men in LA, but I'd never wanted to rip their clothes off the moment I saw them and explore every inch of *their* bodies.

I was incredibly drawn to Kaleb for some inexplicable reason, and it wasn't the sort of attraction I could just blow off.

And God knew that I'd tried.

"I used to come here a lot to fish when I was younger," Kaleb mentioned casually. "My dad was buddies with the old owner. When the acreage came up for sale because the owner was moving to a warmer climate to retire, I was able to buy it to add onto my existing acreage."

We'd ridden a lot of Kaleb's property, and it was expansive. "You don't fish here anymore?"

He shook his head. "Only a couple of times since I've owned it. I don't have a lot of time for hobbies."

"I think you should make time," I teased as I walked down the riverbank. "If I owned this place, I'd be here all the time. It's so peaceful."

"Be careful," Kaleb cautioned gruffly as he followed me. "In those sneakers you're wearing the bank is going to be slick. It's wet out here after the recent snowfall."

Immediately after those words left his mouth, my feet landed on a slippery portion of the bank, and I felt them start to slide. I waved my arms, trying to steady myself, but it was a losing battle.

I let out a panicked squeak as I realized I was about to fall.

Strong arms wrapped around my waist, and I was hauled against Kaleb's massive body before I could topple into the water.

His laugh was warm and deep as he nudged me to a dry spot against a large tree.

"I told you it was slick," he said with a grin as he caged me against the tree like he was trying to keep me safe.

I smiled up at him, but I was still a little rattled from nearly landing in the very frigid water of the river.

"That was close," I said breathlessly.

In a more serious tone, he answered, "I would have never let you fall, Anna. I had your back. I know what it's like out here this time of year."

My body relaxed.

I wasn't used to someone watching out for me anymore. Not since my parents had died, and never this up close and personal.

I'd had a few brief relationships, but nothing like the closeness I felt whenever I was with Kaleb.

He made me feel both giddy with happiness and entirely safe at the same time.

My heart tripped as I felt the warmth of his breath on my face as he leaned closer.

"Are you okay, Anna?" he asked as his gaze caught mine.

No, I wasn't really feeling okay at the moment.

The heat of Kaleb's massive body was getting to me, and I wanted him so much I could hardly breathe.

The warmth and concern in his gorgeous green eyes nearly crushed me.

I wanted to move closer and absorb that warmth. Wallow in it until the iciness I'd experienced inside me since my parents' deaths finally melted completely.

"Kaleb," I breathed on a soft sigh as I wrapped my arms around his neck and stroked the coarse hair at the nape of his neck.

I knew that I was pushing the boundaries of this friendship, but I couldn't stop myself from wanting to get closer to this magnificent man.

"Anna?" he said in a questioning voice, his eyes glued to mine like he was trying to read my actions.

I stared back at him unflinchingly, my eyes pleading with him to kiss me.

I knew it was probably wrong.

Kaleb wasn't attracted to me that way.

But if it was totally wrong to be this close to Kaleb, why did it feel so…right?

Like a man who had suddenly lost his patience, his glorious mouth came down on mine with a bold intensity that briefly surprised me.

He took my mouth like he owned it, buried his hands in my hair and tilted my head until he had access to explore at his leisure.

Bliss flooded over me as I recovered from the shock of feeling those warm lips on mine, and I moaned against his mouth because he felt and tasted so damn good.

God, he knew exactly how to make a woman crazy with lust almost instantly, and I relished the sensations because I'd felt so cold and alone for such a long time.

I felt his kiss from the top of my head to my toes, and loved the way he made me feel.

Needed.

Wanted.

Adored.

Protected.

And madly desired.

He made me long for so much more, but that didn't stop me from enjoying the moment, and the way that Kaleb was kissing me like a desperate man.

I strained to get closer, pressing myself against his hard, muscular body while his tongue explored my mouth possessively.

I wanted to crawl inside Kaleb and never leave, and I couldn't seem to get close enough to take the edge off my almost unbearable hunger for him.

Then, suddenly, he released my mouth with a small groan.

"Fuck!" he cursed hoarsely. "I'm sorry, Anna. That was a mistake."

He backed off until no part of him was touching me, and I was suddenly cold again.

"Was it a mistake?" I asked, my voice trembling with emotion as I leaned against the tree for support.

I'd beckoned.

He'd answered by getting intimately close to me.

And now…he regretted it?

Holy shit! I was an idiot.

For just a moment, I'd felt like he really wanted me, but it was apparently an impulsive gesture on his part. Possibly because my eyes had been begging him to kiss me.

My eyes caught his, and he shook his head. "It won't happen again. It shouldn't have happened once. Jesus! We're supposed to be friends. I'm supposed to be protecting you for fuck's sake."

My heart fell to my feet.

He did regret one of the most amazing things I'd ever felt.

I tore my gaze from his. "It's fine. It's not like I've never been kissed before."

Okay, I *had* been kissed. Plenty of times.

It had just never felt the way it had when Kaleb kissed me.

I'd also never felt this crushed because that very brief, intimate moment was over.

It actually really hurt that he was remorseful about the whole interlude.

"You're supposed to be here to grieve and heal," Kaleb rasped. "It was a stupid move on my part, and pretty damn selfish."

*Selfish?*

That kind of led me to believe he *had* wanted that kiss on some level.

Or maybe that was just wishful thinking on my part.

I opened my mouth to ask, but when I finally glanced at him again, Kaleb looked completely shut down emotionally.

Distant.

Elusive.

Broody.

Not the same Kaleb I knew and adored.

"We'd better head back," he said stiffly. "My mother is expecting us for dinner."

I'd happily accepted that dinner invitation because I really wanted to meet Millie Remington.

He waved toward the horses, indicating that he wanted me to lead the way.

As usual, he was watching my back.

*Let it go, Anna. Maybe it was a mistake for Kaleb.*

Because he acted like he wanted to forget that the kiss ever happened, I stayed silent and headed back toward Bella.

That kiss wasn't an experience I was ever going to forget, but if that was what he wanted, I'd try my best to pretend that it had never happened.

He'd done so much for me.

He'd gone out of his way to help me, and we were friends.

I owed him that consideration.

I'd try to pretend that kiss was nothing.

The problem was, I knew I would never forget being that close to Kaleb, no matter how hard I tried.

## Chapter 11

*Kaleb*

"Let's hope your mom likes me, even though I'm not exactly dressed for dinner with someone I've never met," Anna said as she walked into the kitchen that evening.

She'd been concerned about the casual wardrobe she'd brought with her, but she looked absolutely gorgeous.

I'd told her not to dress up because family dinners were always casual.

She was wearing a pair of dark jeans, and a bright red, flowy blouse that looked stunning on her.

Anna normally didn't use heavy makeup in her daily life, but she'd used a heavier hand with it tonight, and that fuck-me scarlet lipstick she was wearing made her lips even more tempting than they had been earlier.

I was fucked.

My dick got hard immediately, and I had to look away from her to keep myself from kissing her senseless all over again, even though I hated myself for kissing her the first time.

She hadn't really wanted that embrace, but she'd responded so sweetly that I'd been hard-pressed to let her go.

She was vulnerable, and I despised myself for taking advantage of her state of mind earlier.

I'd wanted her, and I'd taken what I wanted without thinking about what Anna might need from me.

Well, that shit wasn't happening again. I had myself firmly in check tonight, and it was going to stay that way.

"You look stunning," I told her honestly. "For Crystal Fork, you're all dressed up. And my mother will love you. Nobody dresses up for a casual dinner here."

I was wearing a pair of jeans and a gray, wool sweater, which was about as dressy as my mother saw from me unless I was heading for the office.

She nodded as she dropped her lipstick in the purse she was using.

Anna had been a lot less talkative since I'd kissed her, and I hated that.

Her less than exuberant mood was even more proof that touching her had been a huge mistake.

I didn't know what I'd been thinking when I'd given in to the urge to kiss her.

I'd looked down at her, felt her shapely body against me, met those killer eyes of hers, and I was completely screwed. There hadn't been a rational thought in my head at the time.

She'd been so damn sweet that I'd lost my shit for a few moments.

However, I had instantly regretted that when it was over and I saw the confused look on Anna's face.

Things between us had shifted after that kiss, and the last thing I wanted was for Anna to be unsure about what she was going to get from me.

It only took us all of five minutes to get to my mother's house once we'd left my property. Anna fidgeted a little as we pulled into the long driveway of Mom's ranch.

"I'm a little nervous," Anna confessed as she fussed with her hair. "I am about to meet a really famous artist."

I chuckled. "You meet far more famous people all the time."

Hell, she was one of those superstars, but you'd never know it judging by Anna's reaction right now.

"That's different," she said anxiously. "They're performers like me."

I laughed this time because I couldn't stop myself.

I didn't mingle with A-listers or music superstars, but if I had to guess, she was probably a rarity, a woman who thought nothing of her celebrity status.

"She's an artist," Anna added reverently when we finally reached my mom's home.

I had to force myself not to laugh again.

Anna was an artist and incredibly creative, too.

Strangely, she didn't think she was anything special even though millions of people adored her and her talent.

"Great," I said drily as I saw the vehicles in the driveway. "My brothers invited themselves to dinner, too."

"That's good," Anna said in a happier tone. "I like them."

"You didn't have to grow up with them," I replied. "I should have known they'd be here if Mom was cooking. They both hate to cook."

Anna laughed for the first time since we'd been out to the river, and it was a sound that made my gut ache.

I'd missed that sound.

*A lot.*

I was starting to depend on hearing her laughter and seeing her smile every day to remind me that life wasn't all about work. Anna also continued to teach me that life didn't have to be serious every single minute of the day.

Granted, we'd discussed some serious topics, but we also laughed together equally as much.

"Don't fuss," I told her as I grabbed the hand messing with her hair. "You look beautiful."

I was starting to realize that messing with her hair was a nervous habit, probably because whenever she went out, she was often being watched by the public.

She rolled her eyes at me as we hit the porch. "You always say that."

"I'll always think so," I shot back.

"Maybe you should start off slow instead of taking her directly to the spring fundraiser," Mom said thoughtfully.

"Like?" I questioned.

"Take her to The Mug And Jug for coffee tomorrow morning. Let some people get used to seeing her with you before you show up at the fundraiser where the entire town will be present," Mom suggested. "Silas will love flirting with her."

"The Mug And Jug?" Anna questioned. "And who is Silas and why would he flirt with me?"

I grinned at her. "The Mug And Jug is the most popular place in town. They serve gourmet coffee in the morning, and then it turns into the only bar in town in the evening. Silas Turner owns The Mug And Jug, and he tries to flirt with every female in town. He's eighty-four years old, and he's harmless."

"Gourmet coffee," Anna said longingly.

I grinned wider, knowing I wasn't going to have to twist her arm to go with me.

"And the best cinnamon rolls in the area," Tanner added as he took a break from his food.

Anna's eyes widened. "I love cinnamon rolls, but they don't love me. Sweets pack weight on me in a hurry, and my stage costumes are already tight. I haven't been watching my diet very closely since my parents died. I've been indulging in too much comfort food. I haven't even looked at a salad in months."

My mother laughed. "I don't see a single extra pound on your body, hon. You can afford a cinnamon roll."

Mom was a little plump, and she always thought everyone else was too skinny, so she always tried to feed everyone, whether they needed to gain weight...or not.

However, she was right to try to get Anna to eat what she wanted. She was curvy in all of the right places, but she was slender. Hell, did her weight really matter in the first place? If she wanted a damn cinnamon roll or two, she should have some.

It sounded to me like she'd deprived herself of way too many of the simple pleasures in life for the sake of her career.

Anna shrugged. "The press is brutal on women in entertainment sometimes. They notice every single extra pound."

Mom shook her head. "Don't ever let anyone tell you that you aren't beautiful, Anna. No matter how much you weigh. External appearances change as you go through life. It's what's in your mind and your heart that makes you beautiful."

"I know that's true," Anna said thoughtfully. "But it's hard to remember that when you work in entertainment. The way you look is everything."

"It shouldn't be," Mom mumbled unhappily. "You play the piano and sing like an angel. That should be more than enough to make people happy."

Anna smiled at her warmly as she answered, "Thank you for the compliment."

She didn't contradict my mother, even though I knew the demands on her because of her profession weren't quite that simple.

It irritated the fuck out of me that Anna was always on display and was expected to be physically perfect at every performance and in every photo or video of her.

I was sure she got criticized all the time, but I wanted to punch every person who had ever said something negative about her.

Mom put her spoon on her empty plate. "Well," she said in an upbeat voice.

My brothers chortled because they knew exactly what was coming, just like I did.

Mom was rarely subtle when she wanted more information.

"Now that we've gotten to know each other a little," she continued. "Let's talk about this so-called friendship between you and my very eligible son."

## Chapter 12

*Anna*

"I completely adore your mom," I told Kaleb as we stood in his kitchen drinking a beer later that night.

We'd stayed at his mom's house until after midnight, and I'd really enjoyed her company.

Yes, she'd grilled me about my relationship with Kaleb, but it had been fairly easy to deny a romantic relationship because it was the truth.

Strangely, Millie didn't have any of her own art hanging in her home. She told me that she would much rather enjoy the work of other artists, and that it was her late husband who had loved to have her work on display. After Kaleb's father had passed away, Millie had eventually taken down all of her own paintings to hang others from various artists she'd collected over the years. We'd spent a great deal of time looking at and discussing her extensive collection of paintings from other artists.

After that, we'd chatted about anything and everything.

Kaleb's mom was an interesting and easy woman to talk to about almost any subject.

"You still adore her even though she kept trying to marry you off to me," Kaleb said wryly.

I snorted. "You can't blame a mother for trying. I think she's frustrated with all of her 'boys' because you refuse to settle down."

I thought it was adorable that Millie still referred to Kaleb, Tanner, and Devon as 'boys.' She had three very wealthy and powerful sons who were in their late thirties and forty, and she still treated them like kids sometimes.

It was also really sweet that those three men treated their mother with a huge amount of respect, even though I was pretty sure they were more accustomed to giving orders than taking them.

"You four are really close," I said after I swallowed a mouthful of beer.

Kaleb nodded. "Even more so since my dad died. We had to find a way to get through that together. It changed the whole dynamic of our family."

"Now that your dad is gone, I think you feel protective of your mom as the oldest son," I said softly.

I didn't have to ask him how he felt. I could see it in the way he interacted with his mother, and I already knew that Kaleb had an enormous protective streak.

"I think all of us do," he said thoughtfully. "Not that she needs our protection. You probably saw that for yourself. She speaks her mind."

She did, and it was one of the things I really liked about Millie. She was extremely kind, but she was also blunt and to the point.

"Why is it that none of you have ever settled down?" I asked curiously.

It wasn't like they didn't have the opportunity. Every single woman on the planet would probably do almost anything to be with one of the Remington brothers.

Kaleb shrugged. "I don't think any of us are totally against having a family, even though Devon swears he'll never get married. You already know I'm married to my work. Tanner came closer than any of us to tying the knot, but he got dumped by his fiancée. Devon spends what spare time he has working on his music and some of his other hobbies. Maybe none of us have ever met the right woman. I think we'd all like to have someone who cares about us for the right reasons, but it's just never happened."

God, I understood that better than most people would.

I found it sad that a lot of women probably only saw power and money when they looked at any of the Remington men.

All of them had so much more to offer.

"Are you really going to take me to The Mug And Jug in the morning?" I asked.

I was dying to see the town that Kaleb had grown up in, and I'd heard a lot of stories about some of the townspeople and businesses at dinner.

"It's probably the best way to test out this plan," Kaleb answered thoughtfully. "Although I'm not crazy about exposing you to anything that could hurt you in any way. And while we're on the subject of you possibly getting hurt, did you call your agent again about him causing rumors in California? I hesitate to call him your friend. If he really cared about you that much, he wouldn't be pushing to see where you're staying. He should know better. You can't trust him that much if you didn't tell him where you were going in the first place."

I sighed. "My relationship with Ray is complicated. I've known him since I was a child. Dad thought the world of him, but I could never get that close to him. We have almost nothing in common, but he does push me to always be the best I can be as a musician and entertainer. I can't call him a close friend, but I trust him because my father did. Sometimes I do feel like he steps over the agent/client boundaries, but I let it go because he was important to Dad."

"What were your parents like?" Kaleb asked. "You don't have to answer that if it's too painful."

I thought for a moment before I answered. "We were close, but not nearly as close as you are to your family. It seems like we spent most of my adult life talking about my career because Dad was working for me. My mom worked as a cashier in a grocery store when I was younger, but she stopped working when they moved to California with me. I made sure they never regretted making that move."

"I'm sure you did," Kaleb replied. "It sounds like they were stage parents to some extent. Maybe not in a bad way, but they were pretty involved in your career."

"That's a fair assessment," I agreed reluctantly. "But they were incredibly proud of me, and I'm not sure that it was all bad. I was still a teenager when my career took off, and I was pretty naïve when I moved to Los Angeles. I was a Montana girl in a big city. To be honest, it was terrifying when my career took off that fast. My parents helped a lot to keep me grounded and less stressed out about everything. They backed off later, once I had plenty of experience. I can't say that they micromanaged my career after I got old enough to make good decisions. Things were really great between us when they decided to retire to Newport Beach. We still got to see each other, and we finally got to talk about something other than my career. They were enjoying their life, and the only thing my dad still managed was my books and investments. He said he needed something to keep him busy when he wasn't out on the water with Mom."

"He was pretty meticulous about it," Kaleb told me as he tossed his empty bottle in the trash. "I still have a lot to review for you, but it looks like he kept good records. I took a quick look this morning after you sent me your files."

"Now that my dad is gone, I'd really like to learn more about my investments," I said honestly. "Ray isn't a financial or investment manager, and I'd like to take that off his hands."

I'd still need a wealth advisor for investments and a business manager, but I wanted to learn some things myself. Things I should have had my dad teach me, but never had the time. It just didn't feel right to me to have Ray handling anything except his responsibilities as my agent.

Now that I was thinking a little more clearly, I knew that was something that needed to be handled as soon as possible.

I was usually on top of everything that needed to be done, but I'd been dragging my feet on giving someone else a responsibility that had belonged to my father.

Kaleb nodded. "I'll teach you the basics. Do you want me to recommend some people you can trust for your investments?"

"Please," I answered gratefully.

We were quiet for a few moments, and it wasn't our usual, comfortable silence.

Now that we'd finished talking about his family and my business, it was like neither of us knew what else to say.

Things had been a little awkward personally between the two of us because of that damn kiss.

I could feel Kaleb's reluctance to get too personal now. He was distant, and I hated it.

Before he'd rocked my world with that scorching hot kiss at the river, we could easily say anything to each other. Now, I felt like we were circling each other carefully.

Maybe I was a little guarded, too. I could hardly tell him that the only thing I wanted from him right now was to get him naked.

I couldn't even look at him anymore without wanting him to fuck me.

Our relationship had completely changed after our trip to the river, and I really missed that closeness and comradery we'd had at the cabin.

Yeah, I'd pretty much *always* been attracted to him. The difference was, I couldn't seem to control it or compartmentalize it anymore.

I'd gotten a small taste of what it was like to be physically close to Kaleb Remington, and my mind went there every time I looked at him now.

*Dammit!*

I wanted to find a way back to where we'd been before. I didn't want things to stay this awkward between the two of us.

"Kaleb," I said hesitantly, not sure how to fix things.

"Just let it go, Anna," Kaleb said hoarsely. "I made an idiotic mistake."

There was that word again.

Of course he knew exactly what I was going to ask. Mentally, we were usually in tune with each other, even if we couldn't seem to talk like we did before.

I had no doubt he felt the same tension that had been brewing between the two of us since that stupid kiss.

My temper suddenly got the best of me. Or maybe it wasn't my temper. I was genuinely...hurt. "I really hate being called a mistake," I said irritably.

"I didn't call *you* a mistake," he said in an equally annoyed tone. "What happened between us at the river was a mistake."

"You kissed me! *Me*, Kaleb, which makes *me* the mistake."

"You could never be a mistake to me. I care about you, and it was a selfish dick kind of thing to do," he said harshly. "You didn't ask for it. You're not even attracted to me. You're vulnerable right now. You've also been through hell. What kind of man takes advantage of that?"

Yes, I was a little vulnerable, and sometimes I felt alone and lonely, but that hadn't been my primary motivation when I'd wanted him to kiss me. I hadn't wanted *someone*. I'd wanted *him,* and I'd known exactly who I wanted to touch me.

"Oh, for God's sake, Kaleb, I *did* want it," I told him, exasperated that he was blaming himself for what happened. Had the infuriating man forgotten that I'd kissed him back very enthusiastically? "Are you really trying to tell me that you couldn't tell that my eyes were begging you to kiss me? Maybe it was a mistake for you, but I will never, ever, regret that moment. No guy has ever kissed me like that. I can stop talking about it after tonight if that's what you want because you regret every moment of that interlude. But I wanted it, and you can stop feeling guilty about it. If you hadn't stopped so abruptly, I probably would have pleaded with you to take me up against that tree and put me out of my misery. I've always been attracted to you. And while we're at it, yes, I am a little vulnerable, but I'm a grown woman, and you're still the hottest man I've ever seen."

I took a deep breath because I'd run out of air.

*Holy shit!* Had I really just vomited all those words to him without a second thought?

I was a pretty even-tempered and patient person most of the time, but...

As much as I adored Kaleb, he could be the most stubborn, irritating man on the planet at times.

While I loved his protectiveness, he needed to realize that I was a big girl, and I was perfectly capable of pushing away anything I didn't want.

And that included...him.

It was crazy that he couldn't see how much I'd wanted that kiss. How much I wanted *him*.

Maybe because he was too busy regretting it and feeling guilty about it.

Kaleb looked at me like he hadn't totally comprehended my rant, his green eyes filled with an emotion I didn't understand. "Are you finished?" he asked huskily.

Obviously, my lust was screwing with my brain. I just couldn't read him as well as I could at the cabin.

"Yeah, I'm done," I said quietly as I tossed my beer bottle in the trash. "I just needed to tell you how I felt. It's utterly ridiculous that you're blaming yourself for something I desperately wanted."

He moved closer until he'd backed me up against the counter. "I'll never forget it, either, and I've been attracted to you since day one, Anna," he growled as he stared down at me, his expression unreadable. "I thought it was a mistake because I was under the impression that I'd crossed a boundary with you that I shouldn't have crossed. You'd also never have to beg me to fuck you. I'd be a sure thing if I thought that was what you wanted, too. But I also respect you and your mental health. You're grieving and emotionally exhausted."

My breath hitched as our eyes met and I saw the sexual desire burning in those beautiful green eyes of his.

"And if I told you that I think you're exactly what I need right now?" I asked softly. "I'm not asking for some kind of commitment or relationship, Kaleb. All I want is you for as long as we can be together. For once, I'd really like to live in the moment and forget that I'm Annelise Kendrick."

He ran a frustrated hand through his hair. "Then I'd say that when you feel whole and healthy again, all you have to do is tell me you still want the same thing. Fuck knows I could never turn down the chance to touch you again, even though I probably shouldn't. My life is here, and yours is in Los Angeles. But I'm willing to take whatever time together that we can get, too, even if you decide you just want to stay friends."

My heart ached, and I wanted to tell him that I was ready right now.

But I honestly couldn't do that.

I wasn't sure I could be with Kaleb without it completely screwing up my head.

This was about more than just sex for me.

I felt a lot more grounded and less empty when I was with him, but I needed to make sure I had my head together, no matter how much I wanted him right now.

Kaleb deserved a whole woman, even if it was just for a little while.

I nodded slowly because I had a lump in my throat that didn't allow any words to come out.

Because I needed to be close to him, I slid my arms around his neck.

His arms wrapped around me tightly, holding me like he'd never let anyone or anything hurt me.

The closeness wasn't sexual.

It was comforting.

God, he was protective with the people he cared about, and it was something I adored about him.

We stayed just like that for a long time before we finally separated and went to bed without another word on that particular subject.

## Chapter 13

*Kaleb*

"Y ou ready for this?" I asked Anna as I parked my truck right on Main Street, across the road from The Mug And Jug.

I turned to her, and she met my gaze with a confident nod.

*Christ!* I still wasn't used to her eyes being blue. It completely changed her appearance for me. I could still see the emotion in her gaze to some extent, but it was heavily masked by those blue contacts.

They were really good contacts. If I didn't know Anna personally, I'd swear the color was natural.

She was dressed in a light blue sweatshirt and an old pair of jeans.

She'd put on some makeup, but she wasn't wearing that fuck-me lipstick she'd put on last night. Her lips were a duller, muted shade. She had a good eye for what would alter her facial features a little. Probably because she'd been trying to disguise her appearance for a long time.

She'd decided earlier this morning to use the full name of Anna Moore because she'd used the alias before, and was used to answering to that name.

"I need coffee," she whined as she opened the passenger door. "You pulled me out of the house before I could get my fix."

I chuckled. She'd had one cup of coffee. I hadn't completely deprived her. "No time. We're getting a late start."

"It's barely eight-thirty," she said grumpily.

I smiled. Anna wasn't a morning person. At least not until she'd had two or three cups of coffee. "Crystal Fork is a ranch and farming town. People get started before the crack of dawn here every single day, and they roll up the sidewalks when it gets dark. If someone wants something we don't have here in Crystal Fork, they go to Billings."

"I guess I'm not in Los Angeles anymore," she joked as she got out of the car.

When we went to cross the road, I hesitated for a moment, second-guessing the whole plan.

Exposing Anna to anyone went against every protective instinct I had.

"I'll be fine, Kaleb," she said as she gently touched my forearm. "I've done this before without being this well disguised. I really want to be comfortable here. I plan on staying for a while."

Hell, I liked that idea, but still…

"And how did that work out all of those other times?" I asked pensively.

She smiled at me. "Sometimes it worked, and sometimes I was eventually recognized. It was always difficult to hide all that blonde hair. It wouldn't fit in a hat, and if I acted like I was deliberately disguising myself, people tended to notice me even more. I look different today, Kaleb. I don't think anyone is going to accuse me of being Annelise."

She was probably right. People might think she looked a little familiar, but she looked so different from her alter ego right now that it would be hard to place where they had seen her before. "I still don't like it," I grumbled.

"Trust me," she pleaded. "If I thought it was that risky, I wouldn't be here. I know you're trying to protect me, but I want to protect you and this town, too. Let's get coffee. I only have one eye open right now."

I let out a heavy breath as we crossed the street.

Anna knew what she was doing, and she really wanted to feel like a regular visitor to Crystal Fork.

It wasn't like she hadn't lived with this shit her whole adult life.

She needed to feel normal, and it was hard to deny her something this important to her.

Besides, *I'd* be here if anything bad happened.

That was better than her being by herself or with someone else when she introduced herself to the town.

I opened the door for Anna, ignoring the familiar clinking of bells that sounded as the door opened.

I was relieved when I saw that only a few tables were occupied when we stepped inside.

The Mug And Jug was a large gathering spot, and it got crowded at times.

I directed her forward and straight to the long, wooden counter that also functioned as a bar at night.

Anna slipped onto a barstool like she'd been to the place a million times.

Silas came out of the back room. He lifted a hand in greeting to me, and then stopped suddenly when he saw Anna.

"You're new here," the older man said as he started to move to a spot right in front of her.

She shot him her sweetest smile. "I am. I'm visiting this lovely town. I heard this is the best place to get an amazing cup of coffee."

Silas shot me a questioning glance before he looked back at Anna with a grin. "You heard right. What will you have?"

"Anything that's packed with caffeine and a lot of frothy milk?" she asked hopefully with a look of longing on her face.

*Jesus!* Was there a guy on the planet who could deny this woman when she asked that nicely?

Not Silas, obviously.

He looked like a man who was instantly smitten with the woman in front of him.

He stroked his silver beard as he beamed at Anna. "I'll fix you up, darlin'. Do you want that coffee as sweet as you are? Not that a pretty girl like you needs any extra sweetness."

Anna fluttered her eyelashes. "Yes, please."

I rolled my eyes. I'd probably heard Silas say those words a thousand times before.

The man never stopped trying to charm any female who walked into his establishment.

"The coffee, Silas, and give her one of your cinnamon rolls, too," I said a little impatiently. "I'll have the usual."

I plopped my ass on a stool next to Anna as I surveyed the people in the room.

I was glad to see that I knew every face in the room. Most of them were enjoying their coffee before opening their businesses at nine.

Yeah, everyone stared, but not any differently than they'd look at any stranger in the small town.

I was still a little edgy, but I relaxed a fraction because no one was looking at Anna like they'd just seen Annelise.

"You finally got yourself a woman, Kaleb?" Silas asked as he started to prepare the coffees.

Silas moved like a guy half his age sometimes, especially when he expertly served up a fancy coffee or a tall glass of beer on tap.

I shook my head as Silas sent me a quizzical look.

*Fuck!* I loved this town and most of the people here, but I occasionally hated the way everyone expected to know my business. "Like she said," I answered shortly. "She's here for a visit."

Anna merrily introduced herself to Silas and explained her cover story about being here for business.

"Silas Turner, young lady," the older man said as he slid a mug topped with whipped cream in front of Anna. "But you can just call me your boyfriend."

Nonplussed, Anna shook her head. "I can't."

I was honestly amazed at how well she could convince people that she was just a normal person.

Hell, maybe that was because she didn't feel like anyone special.

She was laughing at something someone had said when our eyes met.

For a split second, she made me feel like I was the only person in the room before her attention returned to the woman who was speaking.

And I liked the way that felt.

It wasn't just lust between Anna and me, although I'd had a very difficult time not taking exactly what I'd wanted the night before.

The two of us were inexplicably connected in a way I'd never experienced before.

It had occurred to me once or twice that maybe there was a reason I'd been compelled to go to the cabin.

It was a strange thought for me since I was a man who didn't believe in anything that couldn't be proved by real facts or science.

But occasionally, I wondered if the reason I'd gone to that cabin when I did was to meet the woman who was sitting a few feet away from me.

The problem was, now that we'd met, I wasn't sure how in the hell I was ever going to watch her leave.

## Chapter 14

*Anna*

"This must have been painted at the cabin," I said, completely awed as I looked at the painting Millie Remington had donated for the auction.

Kaleb and I had been working at this site since early this morning. The fundraiser was being held in the park right outside of Crystal Fork. Probably because it was the only space large enough to hold most of the town.

The weather was perfect. Warm, without a cloud in the sky.

The work hadn't been all that laborious for me. There had been plenty of muscle to set up tables, and I'd ended up helping Millie organize boxes of items so they got to the right tables.

Kaleb's mother had finally waved the two of us away this afternoon and told us to take a break and check out the food and items for sale.

We'd walked around the event, sampling the baked goods and food, and looking at the booths with handicrafts and other items for sale.

Although people stared at the two of us, I knew they weren't staring because they knew I was Annelise. They were checking us out because they wondered what my relationship was with Kaleb. He and his brothers were probably the most eligible bachelors in Montana.

We'd finally hit the area where items were laid out for the auction.

Millie's painting was on a stand in the middle of the auction area, with other items laid out on various tables around it.

The painting was larger than the one I owned, and I decided immediately that I had to have it. I hadn't gotten outside that much at the cabin after the storm had cleared, but I'd immediately recognized the small valley and some of the trees I'd seen before Kaleb and I had hopped into his helicopter.

"Bluebells In The Valley," I said as I read the title of the work. "I'd say that's pretty appropriate."

The valley was lush and green, dotted liberally with so many bluebells that it was absolutely breathtaking.

No wonder Kaleb's mother and father had loved their retreat so much. Gazing at the picture made me wish I'd been at the cabin when the bluebells were blooming.

"I'm bidding," I told him.

"Don't," Kaleb said in a low voice. "I always win my mother's paintings every year. How do you think I got the ones hanging in my house? I'll gift this one to you if you want it. There's no sense in us trying to outbid each other."

"I'll pay you the winning bid price," I insisted.

"Not happening," he said gruffly. "Take it as a gift or we're getting in a bidding war. And I guarantee that I can afford to outbid you."

I whacked him on the arm playfully. "Why do you have to be so stubborn?"

He grinned at me, and my heart tripped. He looked so gorgeous in jeans and that damn T-shirt that lovingly hugged his muscular body. "I come by my stubbornness honestly," he told me in an amused tone. "You've met my mother, and my father was just as ornery when he had his mind set on something. And I have my mind set on gifting that painting to you right now."

I gave up because I recognized that stubborn look on his face.

"Thank you," I said sincerely. "It would be the most amazing gift I've ever received."

He nodded, obviously satisfied that he'd gotten his way, and we moved on, perusing the other items.

"It feels so strange to be normal like this," I confessed as I fingered a beautiful scarf that was handmade. "Doing normal things."

"You're pretty damn good at being a normal person," Kaleb told me. "Nobody has even questioned your identity."

"I didn't grow up a pop star," I reminded him. "I was just a weird girl who liked music and didn't socialize well with most of my classmates. I told you once that I was always different. I never really fit in well in school. I had friends, but they were different people like me. I wasn't good at sports, and I never tried out for cheerleading. All I really wanted to do was play the piano. I was constantly composing music in my head, even as a child. My mind was always somewhere else, and most kids my age thought I was peculiar."

"You are," Kaleb teased. "But only in the best of ways. You're unique, Anna, and you're talented. I think I'd rather stand out as peculiar than to follow the herd. But I get it. When you're a kid, you just want to fit in."

"I fit in better as an adult," I told him. "A lot of musicians are a little eccentric."

"Like Devon?" Kaleb asked drily.

"He's really talented," I said to Kaleb honestly. "He plays the guitar like a professional, and he's really creative musically."

Kaleb's brothers had dropped by last night, and Devon and I had ended up in the music room after he'd offered to help me with feedback on a song I was writing.

He'd picked up a guitar and sat next to me while I was playing the song on the piano. We'd finally worked out the parts together that weren't quite coming together for me.

"He was a lot like you in school," Kaleb commented. "If he hadn't been so interested in business, I think he might have majored in music in college."

"He certainly has the capability to be a professional musician."

"Just like Tanner could have been an artist and made a good living at it," Kaleb said thoughtfully.

"And you could have been a furniture maker," I observed. "But you all ended up being powerful tycoons instead. Sometimes it's strange how much our lives are forever impacted by our choices when we're younger. I don't think I ever realized just how different my life would turn out when I decided to cut that record in Los Angeles. Now that I look back on it, that was a really pivotal decision. I'm not sure where I'd be if I hadn't done that. I'd definitely still be playing the piano, but I have no idea where Juilliard would have sent me after that."

"You said you have no regrets," Kaleb pointed out.

I shook my head as we walked together back toward the food booths. "I don't really," I answered. "I'd do the same thing all over again if I had the choice, but that doesn't mean I don't miss being a regular person sometimes. If I did have to do it all over again, I think I would lean more toward writing pop music than actually performing on huge tours. I've written songs for other artists, and it's something I love doing. I've never needed to perform a song I wrote myself to feel like I've accomplished something. It's the creative process I love, and then hearing it come to life. That's why I do what I do."

"Wouldn't you miss the attention and adoration?" he questioned seriously. "You have an amazing voice, and Annelise is adored by millions."

I thought about his question for a moment before I answered. "I like being recognized for my accomplishments, but no, I wouldn't miss the craziness of being chased down by the media for a story or being mobbed at an event. And I'd gladly give up being a master of disguise. I think I've always been a private person who was somehow shoved out into the public eye. I've learned to cope, and I love bringing my music to the masses. I'm proud of my success. But there is usually a shelf life for pop stars. I know there are exceptions to that, but a lot of the artists I listened to when I was young aren't even talked about anymore. Female pop stars get older, and we're replaced by someone younger. Before that happens, I'd like to bow out of the touring part of my career and focus on writing music."

"You're only thirty-five, Anna," Kaleb protested.

"I'll be thirty-six in a few months. Maybe I'm at that age when I start to look at my alternatives for the future. I actually want to have a child someday. Since I haven't found a life partner, I'd like to adopt a child, and I refuse to leave a child behind while I go out on the road most of the year," I said honestly.

"You were completely serious about not wanting to do mega tours anymore?" Kaleb asked huskily.

"I'm not sure if that's an option for me right now," I told him. "I want to be financially secure so I can do what I want to do. I'll never make the money I'm making right now doing something else, and I'm totally aware that fame is usually fleeting. I've never deluded myself into thinking that I'd be on top forever. Most pop stars aren't, and I've been lucky. I've had a really good career. I've stayed relevant for seventeen years now."

"So you're looking for a backup plan?" Kaleb asked in a deep, thoughtful baritone. "Even though you're a household name and ridiculously young."

I snorted. "You only think I'm young because you're older than I am. I feel old because I'm looking at the young, talented teenagers and early twenties women entering my field. It takes a lot of energy to do a tour like mine. I used to do it without thinking about it. Now I have to watch every calorie and stay in good shape to do concert after concert. It's physically and emotionally exhausting, and it certainly isn't going to get any easier from here. I'm just being realistic. Maybe I'll stay incredibly popular for years, but I feel like I'm always waiting to become irrelevant. Maybe that doesn't make sense to you—"

"Rationally," he interrupted. "I understand your thinking. I guess I've never considered what it would be like to have a career that could very well have an expiration date."

"Maybe because you're not a female who has to look good to younger people in revealing costumes," I said drily. "Men like you are considered incredibly hot at forty. Women in entertainment usually just get older and less desirable."

"Okay, now I have to disagree," Kaleb said in a low, sexy voice. "Your music has kept you relevant, and you'd be desirable at any age, Anna."

I turned my head and caught his gaze.

My heart somersaulted as I saw the raw heat in his eyes.

I actually believed that he might always find me attractive because we just had that kind of chemistry. "But you don't understand how fickle people in the music business and Hollywood can be."

"Oh, I understand it," he contradicted. "I just don't walk in your shoes. What I look like doesn't really matter as long as my mind is still sharp enough to do business."

"Well, it matters in my business. I'm not a performing artist who's judged only on my talent. I'm a female pop star who gets criticized about my personal appearance if it's not perfect. The same thing happens to actresses and other women in entertainment. Reporters comment on their wardrobes, a wrinkle starting to form on their faces, bags under their eyes, and every pound they gain. We either learn to let it roll off our backs or it will eat us alive."

"Obviously you've learned to ignore it," Kaleb observed as he steered me around a large booth.

"Most of the time," I answered. "It doesn't hurt me anymore. The only thing that still stings is if a new album gets horrible reviews, but I've learned over time that some people are just going to hate my music. There's nothing I can produce to change that."

"Everyone has critics if they put themselves out there for public scrutiny," Kaleb said sympathetically.

"I know," I answered quietly. "And I try not to take it personally anymore. But there are some reviewers that go out of their way to land a few blows. Sometimes a personal comment about my music gets to me. I put my heart and soul into that music, and I'm human."

Kaleb put a strong arm around my waist and squeezed. It was a quick, comforting gesture that made my heart lighter.

I was pretty sure that he wanted me to know that he'd always have my back.

"Nothing wrong with being human," he drawled as he pulled his arm away before anyone noticed.

I sensed that he wanted to say more, but this wasn't the place to have an in-depth discussion about my career.

People were watching, and they'd probably listen if they got close enough.

The Remington brothers were all a source of fascination for some of the people in this town, and I didn't doubt that a lot of gossip probably revolved around them.

"I'm sorry," I said remorsefully. "I was ranting a little about work frustrations, but I know I have it good. I honestly have nothing to complain about."

"We're all allowed to have frustrations, no matter how much money we make," he pointed out. "Money and fame doesn't take away the fact that we all have personal issues and problems. It just makes them a little easier to solve if those problems can be solved with money."

The problem was, money couldn't always make everything better.

I'd known a lot of very famous people with money who couldn't manage to fight their personal demons or their private pain with money.

I bumped his shoulder playfully. "Says the man who has more money than God."

"Unfortunately, I've discovered there are some things even I can't buy," he said in a self-mocking tone.

Tanner and Devon joined us before I could ask Kaleb exactly what he meant.

He was, after all, Kaleb Remington.

What could he possibly want that he couldn't pull out his checkbook and buy instantly?

I laughed as I watched Kaleb, Tanner, and Devon as they jabbed at each other about who had done the most work volunteering.

I tucked my work issues away as I listened to the now familiar banter between the brothers.

Right now, I was going to savor the rest of the day just being an ordinary visitor in Crystal Fork, Montana.

## Chapter 15

*Anna*

"You sound so much better," Kim said about a month later as we chatted on the phone.

"I feel better," I confessed to my best friend.

I'd started seeing a virtual grief counselor at Kaleb's suggestion right after the fundraiser.

I'd seen a counselor right after my parents' deaths, but I'd had to go back on the road to complete my tour.

I'd found someone in Los Angeles who did virtual counseling and was used to working with high profile clients and keeping their secrets.

We'd met three times a week for the last month by video, and even though I had been feeling happier since Kaleb and I had met at the cabin, the specialty counselor was helping me work through a lot of my issues.

She made me feel like all of my feelings were normal and part of the grief process.

Even my mental meltdown after my last concert.

She thought that I had been in denial about my grief in the beginning, and when I'd found out that my parents were murdered, it was a trigger that made everything hit me all at once.

I suspected she was right. I'd stayed so busy that I'd never allowed myself to really grieve my parents right after they'd died.

I hadn't truly dealt with the pain of that loss until I'd absolutely been forced to do it when I'd learned that they were actually murdered.

I hadn't wanted to accept that I'd never see them again or that I was now alone in the world without close family.

"How's that hottie man you're staying with," Kim teased. "Girl, I swear, I don't know how you keep your cool around all those gorgeous Remington men. I dug up pictures of all of them. Billionaires are rarely that hot."

Kim knew everything.

She was one of those best friends who would pull your secrets out of you if you didn't tell her everything.

She was also the one person, other than Kaleb, who I knew would always have my back.

"He's just as amazing as he was a few days ago," I confessed as I sat on the bench for the piano in the music room.

I'd been working, but I'd decided that I needed a break.

Kaleb and I had spent almost every day together for the first few weeks that I was here, but he'd needed to go back to work.

He did come home every night at a very reasonable time, and I'd been fine with staying here alone so I could get caught up on writing my music.

"You sound like you're even crazier about him than you were a few days ago," Kim said, her voice amused. "Maybe you should just seduce the guy."

It got harder every single day for me to push aside my physical attraction to him, even though I valued the friendship we had, too.

He'd left the ball in my court, and I wasn't quite sure why I didn't just tell him that I was ready to take that next step.

He certainly wasn't going to push me to make that decision.

He hadn't kissed me since the river, and when he did touch me, there was always a line for him that he wouldn't cross. I knew there always would be until I told him that I felt like I had my head on straight again.

Lord knew I wanted him more than I'd ever wanted any other man. I was ready, but the words I needed to say just hadn't come out of my mouth yet.

I was fairly certain that once Kaleb had changed our relationship, that it was going to be hell to walk away.

On the other hand, I was probably going to regret it if I never got the chance to find out what it would be like to be intimate with someone like Kaleb Remington.

"I think..." I started hesitantly. "I think I'm nervous."

My relationship with Kaleb meant everything to me, and I wasn't sure what would happen if we ended up having sex.

It would change the whole dynamic of our relationship, a relationship that meant a lot to me.

Kim cleared her throat. "Nervous?" she said in a surprised voice. "You're Annelise. What single man wouldn't want to sleep with you?"

Oh, Kaleb wanted me. I could see that raw desire every time he looked at me, but he hadn't tried to rush me into anything I didn't want to happen.

"I didn't say that he didn't want me," I explained. "But you know how much he means to me, Kim. I guess I'm afraid that it will change the two of us somehow."

"Yeah, you'll both be a lot less frustrated," she answered with a sigh. "Is there some reason why this relationship can't just continue in the future so you can see what happens? You always talk like the two of you have an expiration date."

"Honestly, we do," I said wistfully. "We've never talked about any kind of future relationship. Kaleb's life is here. Mine is in California. I can't stay here forever. You know what my life is like. I'd never expose him to that kind of public speculation and bullshit. His company has an excellent reputation, and he's not a public kind of guy.

If he was constantly dating A-listers and supermodels, I probably would have recognized his face. He and his brothers keep a low profile because they like it that way. They like to keep their private life…private."

"If you care about someone, you make exceptions and compromises, baby girl," she said in her usual, no-nonsense tone. "Has it ever occurred to you that Kaleb Remington might be your perfect match, and that you might be his, too?"

Kim was Kaleb's age, a mother of two, and the owner of a very successful business that she'd built from the ground up.

Generally, she was pretty direct, and she didn't tell me what I wanted to hear all the time.

That was probably why we'd gotten so close over the years.

"Yeah," I admitted. "I've never felt the way I feel when I'm with Kaleb. Not even close. But we've gotten to be best friends, too. There's almost nothing we don't talk about."

"Best friends don't usually want to tear each other's clothes off," she answered drily. "Look, being best friends with the guy you're also sleeping with is the best kind of relationship. It's what keeps a couple together when things get tough. If all you have is lust, your relationship is doomed. It won't last. Trust me. I went through a lot of dramatic, hormone driven relationships before I met the right guy. It's normal to be worried that things will change once your relationship is altered, but you might regret it if you don't find out."

I smiled. Kim and her husband were adorable. They bickered like kids sometimes, but it was always obvious that they were meant to be together.

I'd always desperately wished I could find that kind of relationship myself, but it had never happened.

"I know I'd regret it," I said with a huge sigh. "I highly doubt I'll even feel this connected to someone again. I'm thirty-five years old, and I've never felt this way before."

"You've spent your entire life trying to make other people happy," Kim said gently. "Your parents. Your agent. Other artists. The press. All of your fans. For once in your life, do exactly what *you* want to do. You've lived your life for other people long enough. It doesn't sound like Kaleb wants anything from you but to be with you. That has to feel almost abnormal."

I had to admit, it did feel strange to have someone who probably gave as much or more than I did. He'd even parted with one of his mother's paintings for me just because I'd coveted it.

"He's different than any man I've ever known," I confessed. "But I'm not sure he wants a future with me. Not that way. I think he realizes that we're going to part ways, eventually. I have to be back to perform at the awards ceremony in a few weeks. I'm committed to it. I'm going to have to be in California."

God, I dreaded the day I had to leave, and I'd thought about it as little as possible.

I was happy here in Crystal Fork. Besides the obvious reason, which was Kaleb, I'd also fallen in love with his family and the people here.

I roamed the town, even when Kaleb wasn't with me, and there were friendly faces and conversations everywhere I went.

Millie stopped in fairly often when Kaleb was at work, and I'd took Bella over to visit her ranch. She was such a sweet, motherly kind of woman that it made losing my own mother slightly less painful when I hung out with her.

I also stopped into The Mug And Jug as often as possible.

I'd gotten very fond of Silas, and whether I wanted it or not, he was always there with some kind of advice or kind words.

Basically, I'd learned that Silas Turner was a total fraud. I'd come to suspect that his flirtation was more about making women feel good about themselves than his desire to hook up with any of them. He cared about the people in this town more than he wanted to admit.

"You coming back will make Ray happy," Kim told me in a frustrated voice. "He still hounds me at the salon almost every day. He knows that if anyone knows where you are, it's me."

I closed my eyes, hating myself because my agent was still bothering my best friend because of me. "God, I'm so sorry."

"I'm not," she answered immediately. "He's annoying, but I enjoy messing with him sometimes. That man is full of himself. I know he's a friend, but he's stepping miles over the line right now. It's none of his damn business where you are and what you're doing. You're a grown woman. You've met all your obligations. You lost both of your parents, and you still kept on working until you finally cracked under a tremendous amount of pressure and grief. Have you heard anything from the detective working on the case?"

"Nothing," I replied, frustrated. "I check in with the detective often. They won't tell me much because it's an active investigation, and I don't even know if they have a suspect yet."

"Then I think it's safer if you stay there in Montana. Maybe the police aren't saying it, but it worries me that you could be a target, too."

"Sometimes I wonder if all this has something to do with me," I agreed. "Maybe it's someone who hates me and wanted to get back at me by killing my parents."

It was a horrible thought for me, that my parents could have died because of me or my career. But it wasn't impossible, either. I still couldn't think of anyone who had a beef with my mom and dad.

"It could also be random," Kim said firmly. "I guess we won't know until they get some leads on who did it and why. I just want you to be careful, just in case."

"I'm always careful," I assured her.

"What are we doing with your hair when you come back to Los Angeles?" Kim questioned. "You're performing at the awards show and you're up for multiple awards. You're going to have to do a public appearance almost as soon as you get back. Are you keeping your new look?"

"I guess I should switch things back again," I said hesitantly. "Or get as close as possible."

I'd been such a mess when I'd left California that changing my appearance back to Annelise again had been the last thing on my mind.

"I can color it and do some hair extensions. Your hair won't look exactly like it did before your transformation with your natural hair, but I can make you look like Annelise again."

Honestly, I liked the woman I saw in the mirror now, but people had expectations. I wasn't sure what changing my look would do to my career.

"I wish I could keep my current style and my natural hair color," I confided. "I think I forgot what it looked like. I've been a blonde most of my adult life."

Someone had suggested the change when I'd first broken into the music business, and because I'd become successful, I'd always stayed a very long-haired blonde.

"If that's what you want, do it," Kim said firmly. "You look gorgeous. Personally, I think your natural color and the cut suits you better."

"Not to mention the fact that it's a lot easier to maintain," I mentioned. "I love you, but you know I hate all the hours I have to spend in that salon chair. Keeping up the color, the highlighting, and length was a pain in the ass. All I have to do is blow-dry it now, and getting my hair dry doesn't take forever."

"Then keep the more natural look. Think about it," Kim suggested. "You have some time to make a decision."

"Not that much time," I said pensively.

"Then I guess you better get moving on seducing that gorgeous man of yours," she teased. "Try not to let thoughts of your future color the way you live in the present moment. You sound happy for the first time since your parents died. Wallow in that. Enjoy every private moment you have with Kaleb while you have the chance."

"I will," I promised her.

We said our goodbyes and I disconnected the call.

"What are you really afraid of, Anna?" I asked myself out loud as I settled at the piano to work on a song.

There was probably a simple answer to that question.

I was afraid that once I'd gotten that close to Kaleb, I was probably never going to want to leave.

## Chapter 16

Kaleb

"Devon and I are finished looking everything over," Tanner told me while my brothers and I sat in my office in Billings. "Someone has definitely been syphoning millions from Anna's earnings. Our guess is the same as yours. It's all going to a shell company masquerading as an investment."

My heart sank, even though I'd already known my brothers would see the same thing I had.

Anna had trusted me with the passwords to all of her business accounts, her books, and her investment accounts after I saw something that didn't look quite right in the documents she'd sent me a month ago.

I'd downplayed the possible issue because I didn't want to alarm her for no reason.

I'd asked Tanner and Devon to take a look after I'd done a few weeks of digging into all of her finances for the last decade or so, just to verify my findings.

"On the surface," I started solemnly. "Everything looks okay. The money goes out on a regular basis to what looks like a legit investment. But I noticed that she was actually getting zero returns for that investment, and there's a lot of money that went there in the last two years. The statements were total bullshit when you dig deep enough."

Tanner and Devon both nodded from their seats in front of my desk.

"It's the same red flag we saw," Tanner observed. "I called in a favor and found out the account for that company is empty. Unfortunately, I couldn't find out where all that money went."

My anger increased as I realized that she would probably never see that money again. Anna had been swindled for the last two years. "I couldn't find out who actually owns that company, either," I told my brothers. "I think the documents given to the bank for the account and the owner's identity are all fake."

"I tried to find something to prove the legitimacy of the company, too," Devon commented. "But I couldn't find a damn thing. Everything looked good with her books and investments until two years ago when a lot of money started going out to this company."

I nodded. "I noticed the same thing. There were improvements that could have been made to her investments to boost her returns, but there was nothing that didn't check out until this particular investment started."

"Who was responsible for that investment?" Tanner asked.

"I'm not sure," I admitted.

"Who had the authority to do it?" he questioned.

"As far as I know, her dad did her investing, paid her business related bills, and kept track of her business books. He provided all the info to her business accountant for taxes. Her dad did a creditable job considering that he didn't have the expertise that a professional business manager and wealth manager would have had to do it. And her books are meticulous."

"Fuck!" Tanner cursed. "Do you think her father was ripping off his own daughter?"

I shook my head slowly. "I thought about her parents," I mused. "But Anna would have given them anything they wanted. She gave them millions to retire in style in Newport Beach, and she paid her dad a more than generous salary to manage her business affairs. Everything was on the up and up until two years ago. I think it's more likely that someone convinced her dad to invest in this company for her, and he didn't dig deep enough to see that it was a fraud. He was pretty conservative with her portfolio. Maybe too conservative at times. It must have been someone he trusted or someone very convincing."

"Makes sense," Tanner agreed thoughtfully.

"She still has a lot of money," Devon observed. "But it pisses me off that someone would help themselves to her funds. Musicians work hard and someone like Anna gives up her privacy and most of her normal life to work at her craft. She deserved every penny she made."

It didn't surprise me that my brothers were enraged on Anna's behalf. Both of them adored her, and vice versa.

Frankly, it pissed me off, too. In fact, it infuriated me that some asshole had drained some of the money she'd worked so hard for over the last seventeen years.

I knew what her goals were, and that she'd worked hard all these years to gain her freedom.

Yeah, she still had the wealth to stop touring. Hell, she could stop working altogether and live the life of a very wealthy person with the right investments to keep her cash flowing in.

But the draining of her cash into a shell company needed to stop immediately.

Then she needed the appropriate people handling her wealth, specialists who were used to dealing with millions of dollars for their clients to grow that wealth.

"What are you going to do?" Tanner asked.

"I already stopped the damage by keeping any further funds from going into this particular investment," I replied. "I also tweaked some of her investments to increase her gains. I'm going to help her get her money into the hands of reputable professionals who can be on top of her money all the time. She can't take this on herself. It would be a major suck of her time, and she doesn't have that kind of extra time or the expertise to put that money to work for her in the best ways possible."

"A lot of entertainers aren't that great at managing that kind of money," Devon informed me. "They're right-brained thinkers."

"You're a musician and you handle your own money," I pointed out.

Devon grinned and said cockily, "I'm especially gifted. Besides, music is a hobby for me. I'm primarily a left-brained thinker. I'm essentially logical and analytical."

"Anna is logical," Tanner argued. "And down to earth."

She was both, but I remembered her saying that her head was usually in the clouds because she was so gifted musically.

In my opinion, she had the same gifts that Devon had…in reverse. She was a right-brained person who still had a large amount of common sense.

"I'm starting to wonder if this situation has anything to do with the murder of her parents," I considered out loud.

"Is it possible that Anna's dad was getting suspicious of that investment?" Tanner asked.

I shrugged. "I'm not sure, but it is a possibility."

"Are you going to talk to Anna about all this?" Devon asked.

"Fuck!" I cursed and ran my hand through my hair in frustration. "I should do it immediately, but she seems to be doing so much better. The bags under her eyes are gone. She's not mentally and physically exhausted anymore. I can't even begin to say that she's over what happened to her parents. I'm not sure she ever will be. It's been years, and I think we all still miss Dad. But it seems like she's working through her loss, and that she's accepting that they're gone."

"There isn't a lot more that we can do to catch the person who was ripping her off," Tanner said regretfully. "The police need to get involved, and they need to investigate whether it was a motive for murder."

"I know," I acknowledged. "I'm going to track down the detective handling her mom and dad's murder case before I leave the office today, and I'll notify the feds about what we suspect so they can investigate the shell company. Anna has to know the truth. The authorities are going to have to talk to her, and she deserves to know as soon as possible, but I might give it a day before I tell her everything. I'm taking her out tonight to Charlie's Place for dinner, and then to The Mug And Jug for drinks. I'd rather not spoil that outing for her."

"I'll be at The Mug And Jug," Devon mentioned casually. "A local band is playing there tonight. I'm filling in on guitar for a guy who's got some issues and can't be there. I hope you get Anna out on the dance floor. She's a phenomenal dancer."

I already knew that she could dance extraordinarily well. I'd watched just about every video available on the internet of her performances. She had dancers who performed with her, but Anna was always front and center for her livelier songs. She was at the piano for the slower numbers, and the woman sang and played her heart out like no one was watching. It was sometimes hard to believe that she was nervous or that she dreaded going on stage, but she was a woman who had learned to bury her fears and emotions well to the general public.

I had no idea how she toured and performed nearly every night the way she did. It had to be physically and mentally draining.

If she wanted to stop doing huge tours, I wanted to set her up so she could make that happen immediately.

She didn't need to commit to another exhausting tour. She'd been doing it every year for the last seventeen years now.

"I'll be there to check out the band and Devon," Tanner commented. "I probably won't stay long, but maybe I can get a dance with Anna before I leave."

I gritted my teeth. I actually hadn't known that there was music and dancing at The Mug And Jug tonight. Silas didn't do music there every night, but he hired a local band occasionally to perform. "If she feels like dancing, I'll dance with her," I stated flatly.

Tanner smirked. "Not sure that you can watch any other man put his hands on your woman?"

"She's not my woman," I said.

Logically, she wasn't mine, but that didn't mean I didn't feel protective when it came to her.

Hell, who was I kidding? I was also possessive, even though I had no reason to be, and I'd never felt possessive toward a woman in my entire life.

I'd tried to convince myself that I'd have no reason to object if she wanted another guy to touch her.

We weren't intimate.

There was no agreement between the two of us.

*Nothing.*

It seemed when it came to Anna, my logic flew out the window. I couldn't talk myself out of the way I felt about her, even if it was illogical.

"She's not my woman," I said again as I realized my brothers were looking at me like they didn't believe me.

"I call bullshit," Devon interjected. "You look at Anna like she's the only woman who exists for you. Maybe you don't want to admit it, but you're crazy about her."

"We live two totally different lives," I ground out. "She's here to relax, write some music, and grieve for her parents. We're just… friends."

"Cut the crap with us," Tanner insisted. "We already know how you feel about her."

"She's going home to California in a few weeks," I shared. "She has commitments."

Tanner shrugged. "And you have a private jet that can cover that distance in a very short period of time. You said you were getting your priorities straight, and let's face it, she's a big priority in your life now. And there's nothing wrong with that. If you really want her in your life after she leaves, you have the means to make it happen."

"It's not going to happen," I said irritably.

"So you're just going to give up on Anna?" Devon questioned.

"I think if I found a woman like her, I'd move mountains to keep her," Tanner added. "Even if it had to be a long distance relationship."

"I have no idea what I'm going to do," I said, frustrated. "Hell, I don't even know if she wants to keep in touch after she leaves. She's never mentioned it, and we haven't really discussed it."

"For fuck's sake, Kaleb, open your eyes," Tanner said in a disgusted voice. "It's obvious that she cares about you, too."

"We met under bad and unusual circumstances for her," I reminded him. "This has never been a normal relationship. She needed me. I was there for her. Things are going to change. She's feeling a lot stronger now."

Yeah, Anna and I were physically attracted to each other, but I wasn't sure that was going to last for her, either.

Once she got back to Los Angeles, she'd have men trampling each other to get next to her again.

"You're happier than I've ever seen you when you two are together," Tanner said. "No offense, bro, but I think you needed her, too, and I don't think that's temporary."

I didn't argue with him.

He was right.

I'd needed Anna as much as she'd needed me.

She'd given as much to me as she'd taken from me.

Unfortunately for me, in my case, I already knew that the way I felt about Anna was definitely *not* temporary.

## Chapter 17

*Kaleb*

"These drinks are really good," Anna said cheerfully as we sat at The Mug And Jug. "It's hard to believe that they really have that much alcohol."

The two of us had to speak loudly to be heard over the music.

I shot her a concerned look from across the small table. "Take it easy on those MJ sluggers. Believe me, they *are* packed with alcohol, and almost no cola."

She licked her gorgeous lips after taking another sip. "They taste pretty harmless. I like them."

I chuckled. "You aren't going to like them when you wake up tomorrow with a gigantic hangover."

She was on her second one, and the MJ slugger, a Mug And Jug specialty, was notorious for putting grown men under the table.

It was similar to an alcoholic iced tea with rum, tequila, vodka, gin, triple sec, and a tiny dash of cola. The taste was deceiving because of the syrup they added.

The glass they used for the specialty cocktail was enormous, so it actually was a very large amount of alcohol in one drink.

I'd warned her about the alcohol content several times before she'd ordered the first one.

Luckily, she'd filled her belly with food at Charlie's.

Anna wasn't a big drinker. She'd drink a beer or a glass of wine, but she usually preferred her coffee the majority of the time.

She wasn't accustomed to a lot of hard alcohol, but she'd heard about the slugger from Silas and people around town, and had wanted to try it.

"I think I'll switch to coffee after this one," she said with a frown. "I'm not tasting it, but I think I'm feeling it."

Oh, I was sure she *was* feeling it. Even though I was drinking a beer on tap, I'd had many of those sluggers over the years.

"Are you going to ask me to dance?" she asked with a flirtatious smile I'd never seen before. "The band is really good."

*Shit!* She was already tipsy. Dancing was probably a good idea right now. She didn't need to down the rest of that second slugger right now.

I wasn't much of a dancer. I didn't get drunk enough to cut loose on the dance floor and dance like nobody was watching anymore.

In this town, *everyone* was watching, and I was always aware of that.

I stood.

It was a slow song.

I could handle that.

I leaned down close to her ear. "Let's dance."

She batted her eyelashes at me flirtatiously. "With you? I'd love to, handsome."

Okay, she was *definitely* tipsy. Anna had never been this flirty. Not with me, anyway.

She rose from her chair, and it hit me for about the millionth time tonight just how stunning she looked in her navy and white dress and heeled sandals.

Her look was casual. The Mug And Jug wasn't the place for formal clothing, but she looked casually elegant with her long, dangly, silver earrings and matching stacked bracelets.

When I'd seen her come downstairs in a dress, I'd been glad that I hadn't put on jeans, which was my usual town attire. Instead, I'd opted for casual pants with a button-down, green shirt.

"Whoa," she said as she gripped her chair. "I'm a little dizzy."

"Do you want to sit back down?" I asked, concerned.

She beamed at me. "No. I want to dance with the handsomest man in the room."

Okay, well, in that case... "Hang onto me," I said as I wrapped an arm around her waist and guided her onto the dance floor.

People could think whatever the hell they wanted.

I wasn't about to let her go.

She wasn't shy about plastering her sultry body against mine as she wrapped her arms tightly around my neck.

I tightened my grip around her waist, making it clear to every man in the room that she wasn't open to any other dance invitations.

"This is nice," she said with a happy sigh as she put her head on my shoulder when I started to lead her slowly around the dance floor.

*Nice?*

It was more like heaven and hell combined for me.

I loved being this close to her, and inhaling her sweet, familiar scent. But my dick was so damn hard it was almost painful.

The way I wanted to claim her like a damn caveman was unprecedented for me, and holding her in my arms was a temptation that made my gut twist.

Maybe I was a damn masochist, but being this close to her was also something I wanted, painful or not.

"The only thing that would make this better is if both of us were naked and alone right now," she said in a husky, lust laden tone.

My dick twitched. "Christ, Anna!" I said hoarsely. "You should never say that to a man in a crowded place."

I knew it was the alcohol talking for her right now, but that didn't make it any easier for me to hear.

"I'm not saying it to just *any* man," she protested. "Just to you."

*Fuck!* Her saying *that* made it even worse.

"I want to be with you, Kaleb," she said mournfully. "I'm not asking for a future or a commitment. I just want to know what it's like to be with a man I care about the way I care about you. You left the timing up to me. I'm telling you what I want right now."

I swallowed the damn lump in my throat.

A month ago, we were becoming friends with a phenomenal physical attraction.

Now, I was completely obsessed with making this woman mine.

She hadn't even hinted that she wanted to be more intimate in the last month, not since right after I kissed her.

I'd thought that was probably a good thing.

Even though I cared about Anna, we were from completely different worlds.

She'd go back to her life as Annelise, and I would go back to the much lonelier existence I'd lived before I'd met her.

It was the way things *had* to be.

My main goals when I'd invited her here were to see her relaxed, happy, and ready to return to California.

I was accomplishing those goals much faster than I thought possible.

Wait! That wasn't quite true. *Anna* was accomplishing those goals because she was so damn strong and resilient.

"Is that alcohol talking for you, sweetheart?" I said drily.

"No," she said insistently. "Maybe it's made me braver, but I know what I want. I just want…you."

*Fuck!* I wanted her, too, but not like this.

"That's not going to happen tonight, Anna," I grumbled.

Hell, it was probably never going to happen, even though my cock was screaming in protest at the moment.

She lifted her head from my shoulder and looked at me. "It doesn't have to happen right this moment, but I wanted you to know that I hope you feel the same way you did a month ago."

Actually, I…didn't.

A month ago, I'd wanted her more than any other female on the planet, and we'd been friends.

Now, I knew I'd be screwed if I claimed her gorgeous body. She'd be mine.

Since the two of us being together was impossible, I had to keep myself in check.

"It's a rule for me that I don't fool around with drunk females," I grumbled.

"My feelings aren't going to change, Kaleb," she said in a serious tone. "I want you, and I think you still want me."

Oh, hell. I heard the vulnerability in her voice and it nearly broke me. Maybe we couldn't take this relationship beyond the point of friends, but I never wanted her to think it was because I didn't want her.

I moved my hand to the small of her back and brought her pelvis closer to me. "Feel that?" I rasped against her ear.

I'd never wanted to hide how I felt about her, but we'd never had a really frank and dirty discussion about it, either.

Her eyes widened. "Yes," she said with a small moan as she pressed even closer.

"That's how it is for me every time I'm in the same room with you, Anna. I see attractive women often, but they don't make my cock instantly hard the way you do. There's always been something about you that makes me absolutely crazy. Just you."

She smiled as she kept her gaze locked with mine. "I feel the same way. Being with you has always felt right, even when we barely knew each other. Maybe that doesn't make sense, but I really don't care. I've stopped trying to figure out why I desperately need you to fuck me senseless."

My eyes closed, and I pulled her head back to my shoulder.

Maybe those seductive eyes were currently blue, but I still couldn't stand to see the need in her eyes without wanting to sate it.

It killed me.

"You obviously don't want to talk about this," she said, not hiding the longing in her sexy voice.

"Not right now," I said in a graveled voice.

If she told me that she wanted me to fuck her one more time, I'd end up carrying her out of here like a possessive caveman.

I was barely holding onto my sanity right now.

"Okay," she said agreeably. "What should we talk about?"

After that brief and tantalizing discussion, I wasn't sure I could get my mind off our former topic.

"Devon's playing is incredible," she commented. "Does he play with this band often?"

My tense body relaxed a fraction. "Hardly ever," I replied, relieved that she'd moved to a safer discussion. "Only when the guitar player can't make a gig. He's always willing to substitute for any guitar player for any band. It's weird, but he's always been able to switch styles to suit the circumstances."

"So he's basically a chameleon when it comes to styles and genres?" she asked curiously. "That's hard to do."

"I would think so, but he likes and plays all kinds of music."

"Why do you think Tanner left so early?" she asked. "He was here briefly, and then he was gone."

I was fairly certain I knew exactly why Tanner had left so abruptly, not that he ever lingered all that long at the bar.

"Do you remember when I told you that Tanner had come closest to getting married once?" I asked her.

She nodded against my shoulder. "Yes."

"The woman who dumped him moved back to town very recently. She's here. He says he doesn't care. He said it's water under the bridge that happened a long time ago, but I think it still bothers him to run into her."

"Oh, my God. Do you think she's taunting him? Where is she?" Anna questioned urgently, her words slightly slurred from the alcohol she'd consumed.

I subtly pointed her out.

"She's really pretty," Anna commented as she squinted to see the female across the room. "But she's obviously a viper. She has a lot of nerve coming back here after she dumped a good man like Tanner.

He should have stayed and danced with every pretty girl here just to show her that he's moved on."

"I agree," I told her. "But that's not Tanner."

"You're right. I don't think he'd ever deliberately be an asshole to anyone."

Oh, Tanner could be a manipulative businessman at work when he needed to be, but she was right. In his personal life, Tanner wasn't a vindictive kind of guy.

It was interesting just how well Anna had gotten to know my brothers and their personalities within a relatively short period of time.

She had a talent for listening and reading people. One of the things I'd liked about her from the very beginning was her intuitiveness.

Anna had managed to reach past my defenses fairly easily at the cabin, and I wasn't an easy man to get to know.

The slow music ended, and the band announced that they were taking a break.

I led Anna back to the table so she didn't fall face first to the floor and carefully sat her back down in her chair.

Despite her earlier comment about having coffee, she tossed back the remainder of her second slugger in a few gulps.

If I didn't know her better, I'd think that she was nervous.

Time ticked by as she looked around the room, seeming interested in her surroundings.

All I did was watch her.

Something was wrong with her. Something other than the fact that she was intoxicated.

She finally turned her head and looked at me.

My gut clenched as I saw a tear roll down her cheek. She leaned closer so I could hear her. "I'm sorry. I shouldn't have said anything about the way I feel or how much I want you. I know you're physically attracted to me, but I feel like you really don't want anything else to happen between the two of us anymore. I get that, actually. I'm leaving soon, and—"

"Anna, stop!" I growled as I rose to my feet. I couldn't watch her cry for another fucking second. "Nothing you ever say to me is wrong."

I lifted her out of her chair since I knew she wasn't going to be steady on her feet.

Instinctively, she wrapped her arms around my neck so she'd be balanced in my arms. "Kaleb!" she squeaked. "What are you doing?"

"Taking you home," I rumbled irritably.

I'd never actually seen Anna cry. She'd sobbed out her sorrows that first night in the dark, but I'd never had to see those tears in the darkness.

Now, I could see the tears, sorrow, and remorse on her beautiful face, and it wrecked me.

I didn't hesitate as I headed for the exit.

Someone opened the door for me, and I strode through it, my only objective to get Anna home.

She didn't like being vulnerable, and I was going to make damn sure that no one saw that vulnerability except me.

## Chapter 18

*Anna*

I woke up the next morning feeling like someone had repeatedly hit me on the head with a sledgehammer.

I moaned as I sat up slowly and looked at the clock.

*Shit!* It was almost noon, and I still didn't feel like getting out of bed.

I should have listened to Kaleb last night.

Those sluggers had snuck up on me. They'd gone down so smoothly that I didn't notice that I was inebriated until all the alcohol hit me all at one time.

I noticed a tiny thermos, a mug, a large glass of water, some pills, and a blueberry muffin sitting on my bedside table.

I would have smiled if my head didn't feel it was exploding.

*Kaleb.*

He'd obviously done the delivery to my room this morning because he knew I was going to feel like crap.

I downed the pills with some water, and then reached for the small flask.

As soon as I unscrewed the cap, I recognized the scent of one of Silas's specialty coffees, and I already knew the muffin was from

Charlie's. I'd had one before when I was in town, and I'd mentioned to Kaleb how much I loved it.

I filled the mug and started to drink the coffee.

I was slightly queasy, but it wasn't bad enough that I felt like I was going to throw up.

My main problem was the excruciating headache I was experiencing and some major brain fog.

I tried to remember what had happened the night before as I drank the coffee and slowly ate small pieces of the muffin.

I clearly remembered eating at Charlie's and going to The Mug And Jug afterwards, but the details of our time at the bar were a little sketchy after I'd finished that first slugger.

I vaguely remembered Kaleb getting me up to dance. That's when all that alcohol had hit me.

I only recalled little flashes of the events after that, and I wasn't sure if I'd imagined those things or if they were fact.

Clearly, he'd helped me upstairs. I was in my regular pajamas, sleep shorts and a T-shirt. I didn't remember changing my clothes, but I vaguely recalled Kaleb helping me into my bed.

*Shit!* What had possessed me to drink that much hard alcohol? I wasn't a drinker, and I was a lightweight, even with wine or beer.

Yes, I'd wanted to try the cocktail because it was iconic in Crystal Fork, but I hadn't needed to drink the entire thing and then order another one.

Maybe I'd momentarily lost my mind because it was killing me to be with Kaleb without wanting more.

*So. Much. More.*

I'd been a little edgy when a number of pretty women had stared at him when he'd walked into the bar.

Kaleb might not be interested in the single women in town, but they definitely noticed him.

What healthy female wouldn't notice Kaleb Remington when he was around?

He was gorgeous, wealthy, and had a commanding presence that drew every female gaze in the room. He also had a droolworthy, naturally ripped body that came from working outdoors rather than a gym.

Yeah, he spent a lot of time at work, but he was in the barn with the horses every evening, tossing around heavy masses of hay and grain, and tending to some of the barn work himself.

He also helped the local ranchers and farmers whenever they needed it.

Kaleb wasn't a guy who was averse to getting his hands dirty as often as necessary, and his dirty, sweaty look made me think about exactly how he'd look after burning up the sheets in bed for several hours.

I couldn't help it, and it had irritated the hell out of me when I knew I wasn't the only woman in Crystal Fork who thought about *that*.

He was, after all, single and available.

A single woman would have to be crazy not to think about what it would be like to be with a man like him.

I guess I'd needed a drink at The Mug And Jug to chill me out.

However, I hadn't needed to drink *that much*.

I was paying for my utter foolishness today, and it sucked.

Doing stupid things was something I generally avoided. I'd probably done more ridiculously dumb things in the last several weeks than I'd done in my entire life.

I stayed regimented.

Focused.

I had to in my field.

I usually had a million things to do and not enough time in the day to accomplish everything that had to be done.

"Get up, Anna," I grumbled to myself. "You don't get a free pass for the day just because you were stupid enough to get drunk."

By the time I got to the shower, I was feeling a little better.

The pills were obviously helping. The pounding in my head was reaching a lower level, but I still felt like my mind was foggy.

I made my shower quick, brushed my teeth, and threw on a pair of jeans and a comfortable purple T-shirt.

I gathered up the dirty glass, mug, and the thermos to take downstairs to the kitchen.

I was going to need more coffee to make it through the day.

It was Saturday, and Kaleb and I had planned on riding this afternoon.

I hated myself for drinking so much last night because I wasn't sure I was up to getting on Bella today, and riding was one of my favorite activities.

I moved slowly down the stairs and into the kitchen, where I found Kaleb making himself a sandwich.

He was slightly sweaty and I could see particles of dust on his face.

Obviously, he'd been outside working while I was conked out with a hangover.

He looked up as soon as he heard me come into the room. "You okay?" he questioned with a concerned look on his handsome face.

"Other than the fact that I feel like an idiot," I muttered as I put the dishes I'd brought down into the dishwasher. "I think I'll live."

"I should have cut you off after the first slugger," Kaleb said like he was actually irritated with himself. "I know how lethal they can be."

I shook my head. "I'm a big girl. I'm responsible for my own actions, and I do remember the part where I insisted on that second one. You warned me plenty of times. It was a dumb thing to do. Now that I know what it feels like to have a horrible hangover, I'll never do it again."

I moved to the coffee machine as Kaleb asked, "You've never had a hangover?"

"Not like this one," I shared as I started making myself a latte. "I've gotten tipsy several times at events, but I cut myself off so I don't make a fool of myself in public. Please tell me that I didn't act like a total idiot last night. I don't really remember that much about what happened after we got up to dance."

"You didn't," Kaleb said readily as he put a second sandwich on a plate for me and put it on the kitchen table. "You only spoke to me."

I groaned. "How many idiotic things did I say to you?"

He hesitated for a moment. "I didn't take anything you said seriously. You were drunk, Anna. You'll hear about it, so I will admit that I carried you out of there because you weren't steady in your heels. But it was no big deal. Grown men get helped out of The Mug And Jug after overindulging in those sluggers."

I slapped a hand over my face in mortification, and then regretted it because my head still hurt. "Oh, God, everyone saw you carry me out of that bar?"

Kaleb nodded as he put his sandwich on the table and then grabbed some chips from the pantry. "Like I said, it was no big deal. It happens all the time on the weekends there."

"It doesn't happen to me," I insisted. "I've never had to be carried out of a bar because I was so drunk I couldn't walk. I'm sorry. That never should have happened."

I automatically made Kaleb a coffee, too, because I knew he'd drink it with his lunch.

"Don't apologize for having a couple of drinks after dinner, Anna," he told me firmly. "There probably aren't many adults in this town who haven't had one of those sluggers at some point in their lives. I should probably take a shower before we eat."

I motioned for him to sit, letting him know that I didn't care if he was a little sweaty. He hadn't planned on showering before eating until I'd shown up.

I started to relax a little. Maybe people did cut loose on the weekends in town. "Have you?" I questioned as I put Kaleb's coffee next to his plate and sat down in front of my sandwich.

He shot me a sheepish grin as he sat down at the table. "More than once when I was younger. Tanner and Devon have, too."

I lifted a brow. "And did you need to be carried out of the bar?"

"Nah," he answered. "I think I made it out on my own steam, but my brothers had to keep me steady on the way out."

I let out a long sigh. "Okay, that makes me feel slightly less ridiculous, but I could do without this stupid hangover."

"You're doing better than I thought you would," Kaleb admitted as he watched me pick up my sandwich. "At least you're eating. Headache?"

I nodded slowly as I chewed and swallowed. "Bad headache. Thanks for leaving me everything I needed at the bedside. I'm not sure I would have made it downstairs without those things. Now tell me exactly what I did and said that I can't remember."

He eyed me a little warily. "What do you remember?"

"The last thing I have a clear memory of is standing up to dance and being hit by all that alcohol at once," I confessed remorsefully.

He shrugged. "Not much happened after that. We danced, you finished your second drink, and I helped you get back home."

"I was in my pajamas when I woke up. Did you help me with that, too?" I questioned curiously.

"A little," he told me. "It's nothing I didn't see when I stripped you down at the cabin. You managed most of it yourself. I made sure you were in bed before I left your bedroom. You were out almost from the time your head hit the pillow. You have the cutest little snore I've ever heard when you're drunk."

I cringed. I'd probably snored like a drunken sailor, but Kaleb would never tell me that. "That couldn't have been pretty," I said, embarrassed to think about how I'd looked passed out on the bed like that.

He shot me a teasing grin. "You look beautiful, even when you're inebriated."

I shot him a small smile. I couldn't help it. "And I think you're full of crap, Kaleb Remington."

There was nothing attractive about an obnoxiously drunk female.

"What else did I babble on about?" I asked, almost nervous to hear what I'd said in my intoxicated state.

He had a mischievous look on his face when he answered, "Do you really want to hear about that?"

"Yes," I said immediately.

"When we were dancing, you did say you wished we were naked. You also mentioned that you were ready to have sex with me," he said with a chuckle. "Don't worry, I didn't take any of that seriously."

I had to force myself to swallow the bite of my sandwich in my mouth.

*Shit! Shit! Shit!*

I could tell by his expression that he wasn't joking.

I really had said those things to him last night.

"Hey, don't sweat the things you said," Kaleb said in a soothing tone. "It was the alcohol talking."

I nodded without saying another word and took a sip of my coffee.

Maybe the alcohol had made those words slip out of my mouth when my guard was down, but I was sure everything I'd said was true.

I just hadn't been able to talk about it when I was sober.

*Holy shit!* I'd finally gotten up the nerve to tell Kaleb Remington that I wanted him, and he hadn't believed a single word I'd said.

## Chapter 19

*Kaleb*

By the time I turned off the movie we'd been watching that evening, Anna was fast asleep on the couch.

She'd closed her eyes about an hour into the movie, and she hadn't stirred since.

Luckily, she'd seen the movie before, so it didn't matter that she had missed the end of it.

I shut the TV off and tossed the remote on the side table.

Anna had been quiet all day.

I wasn't sure if she was wiped out from her hangover or if I should have kept my mouth shut about the words she'd said the night before when she was drunk.

I would have avoided the whole subject if she hadn't asked me outright what she'd said last night.

Because we were friends, I couldn't lie to her.

Hell, I'd tried to make light of her comments, but I could tell by the look on her face that she'd been upset about it.

We'd skipped riding this afternoon because she was still a little under the weather.

Instead, I'd done some more work in the barn and Anna had read a book most of the afternoon.

I'd gone into town to grab a pizza this evening, and we'd settled down to watch a movie.

She'd been feeling better by the time we'd turned on the movie, but she must have still been feeling the effects of her hangover because she'd fallen asleep, and she never did that during a movie. Even if she had seen it before.

I got out of my recliner and walked over to the couch where she was sleeping.

"Anna," I said as I picked her up. "I'm taking you to bed."

She instinctively wrapped her arms around my neck and sighed. "Is the movie over?" she said, her voice a little confused. "I'm sorry. I guess I fell asleep."

I grinned down at her. "You fell asleep over an hour ago."

"Damn," she said as she opened her eyes and looked back at me. "I missed the end. That's my favorite part."

"You've seen it before."

She nodded sleepily. "Yeah, but I wanted to see it again. Put me down, Kaleb. Are you planning on lugging me up that long flight of stairs?"

"That's the plan," I told her, ignoring her request to put her down. "I did it last night."

Anna was a lightweight. I might be getting older, but it wasn't a burden to carry her small form up the stairs.

"Yeah, well," she said in a disgruntled voice. "I wasn't coherent last night. I missed the whole thing."

I stopped at the entrance to the living room, and Anna turned off the light like we'd done this same thing a million times before.

Sometimes it felt like we had. We were so in tune with each other at times that it felt like I'd known her all my life.

Hell, I wasn't sure what I was going to do when she wasn't around every day.

I'd gotten used to being with her so damn quickly that it wouldn't feel right when she was gone.

As a single guy, I'd never really been lonely without a woman around.

Then again, I'd never met a woman like Anna.

I carried her upstairs, put her down on her bed, and got her pajamas from the bathroom.

She took the pajamas from me as she said, "You don't have to take care of me anymore, Kaleb. I'm fine."

She looked more awake as she got up and went to the bathroom.

Anna came back seconds later dressed in her skimpy sleep shorts and T-shirt.

"We have to talk about something," I told her as she climbed into bed. "But we'll discuss it tomorrow."

"What?" she asked as she looked up at me. "I'm awake now. Tell me."

I sat down on the side of the bed.

Hell, now probably wasn't the ideal time to discuss her finances, but I'd waited all day because she'd been trying to recover from her hangover.

I explained what had happened with the shell company and her investment in that entity.

I also told her what I'd done about it.

Tomorrow was Sunday, but she'd probably start getting calls from the authorities bright and early Monday morning.

She needed time to digest the information before she was overrun with questions.

When I'd finished telling her everything, she looked confused.

"None of that makes sense," she said, her expression puzzled. "My dad was always so careful with my investments. Why would he get involved with a company that wasn't legit? Was it a lot of money?"

"Quite a lot over the last two years. Luckily, it was a later investment, but he put a few million into that company. I'm sorry, Anna. I doubt you'll ever see those funds again. But you have plenty of money, and your dad did well with most of his investments. I tweaked your portfolio to get you a little better return on your investments, and you can stop doing those huge tours whenever you want."

I went over the figures briefly, telling her exactly what she had and in what kind of investments.

"I'll show you more on the computer tomorrow," I promised.

"I'm not upset about the money that was lost. There's nothing I can do to change what happened," she said earnestly. "I'm more worried about why it happened. Do you think Dad knew before he died?"

"That's a question I really wish I had the answer to," I admitted. "I looked over all your financial history, and it didn't make sense to me, either. The investment looked odd, which is why I asked for all your passwords to dig into it further, but I still don't have all the answers. Your dad was a conservative investor. I'm not sure what prompted him to invest in a company that had no financial history. My guess is that he got a tip from someone he trusted, and he thought it would boost your returns."

"Do you think he found out the truth? Do you think that's why my parents were killed?" she asked hesitantly.

I wrapped my arm around her waist and pulled her closer to me. "I'm not sure, sweetheart. It is possible."

I wasn't going to blow smoke up Anna's ass. There was a good chance that the murders had something to do with that shell company. They'd taken in millions from Anna. People had killed for a lot less.

And she was an intelligent woman.

Maybe she wasn't a financial wizard, but she'd put together the pieces of the puzzle very quickly.

"Did the detective sound interested in that information?" she asked as she leaned her head on my shoulder.

"Very interested," I said truthfully. "I have a feeling they weren't sure what direction to go on the case since your parents had no enemies."

"There's nothing to help them," she murmured against my shoulder. "No unknown DNA. No motive."

I knew that Anna talked to the detective often, but they never seemed to have new leads. If they did, they weren't telling anyone about them.

I couldn't blame them for that. They needed to play their cards close to their chests. Anna had never been a suspect because she'd been away on tour at the time, but it was a double homicide. The police weren't going to comment on it until they had made an arrest.

"The feds are going to want to ask you some questions about the shell company you were invested in," I warned.

She looked up at me, her expression a little panicked. "I don't know anything. Dad actually never mentioned that investment to me specifically. God, I wish I knew more, but I don't."

"I know," I said calmly. "Just tell them the truth. You're the victim here, Anna. Not a suspect."

Her body visibly relaxed. "I still feel like an idiot because I didn't know I was invested in a shell company."

"Obviously, your father didn't, either," I pointed out. "It's not your fault. Someone put a lot of effort into covering their tracks. Get some sleep, Anna. We'll go over your portfolio tomorrow when you can actually see those investments. Now that the financial bleeding has been stopped, you'll recover that money in gains, eventually. I'm glad it only went on for two years. I wish it had never happened, but it's hard not to make a few mistakes when you're investing."

"Have you ever made a mistake?" she asked doubtfully.

"A few," I admitted. "It's hard to be in my business and not pick a few losers. It happens to most people who invest. You just have to pick a lot more winners than losers. Your dad was pretty savvy, Anna, and he usually stayed away from anything the slightest bit risky. He did well except for that investment. I don't like the fact that money was sucked from you by a fucking thief, but luckily, you have the money and assets to absorb the loss."

"Thank you," she said softly.

"It was no big deal," I informed her.

"No," she said adamantly. "It's a very big deal. Don't blow this off, Kaleb. You spent a lot of time going through my financial records. If it wasn't for you, it would have been a while before anyone found the financial drain, and this could be connected to my parents' murders. To me, it's a huge deal. It's a debt of gratitude that I'd like to repay somehow, but what do you give a billionaire who has everything he wants."

Actually, I didn't have *everything* I wanted.

The one thing I wanted the most couldn't fucking happen.

"You'd do the same for me if I needed help," I said as I finally stood up.

It wasn't possible for me to see that pleading look in her eyes and not give her anything she wanted.

The problem was, she couldn't give me the only thing I really wanted right now.

I wanted *her*, and *she* was something all of my fucking money could never buy.

It was also something I couldn't ask from her.

I'd decided it was probably better if we never explored the powerful attraction between the two of us.

She *was* going to be leaving shortly.

She'd informed me about her departure without a word about seeing each other after she left.

"Kaleb?" Anna called after me as I reached the door.

I turned around to look at her. "Yeah?"

I really needed to leave the room before I threw all my common sense aside and persuaded her to delve into this almost irresistible chemistry we had.

And to hell with the consequences down the line.

She opened her mouth to speak, and then closed it again.

"Goodnight," she finally muttered.

I nodded and left, almost certain that wasn't what she'd meant to say.

# Chapter 20

*Anna*

I woke up the next morning angry with myself for not saying what I'd wanted to say the night before.

When he'd been ready to leave my bedroom, I'd wanted to tell Kaleb that he should have taken everything I said seriously at The Mug And Jug, even though I was intoxicated.

But once again, the words hadn't left my lips.

It really wasn't like me not to say whatever I wanted to Kaleb, but when it came to my feelings toward him, it was almost impossible to get those out of my mouth.

What if he didn't feel the same way he had weeks ago?

What if he now thought it was better if we just parted friends?

I'd spoken to Kim earlier in the day, and she'd given me hell for not speaking up.

She was right.

None of us was guaranteed a tomorrow or another chance to say what they wanted to say.

God, I knew that better than anyone else. I'd lost both of my parents in one day, and I'd never had that one last chance to say goodbye or tell them how much they meant to me.

I should have said exactly what I was thinking to Kaleb.

He'd done everything possible to let me know he cared about me.

I didn't have any reason to doubt that he had feelings for me, just like I did for him.

Maybe he had changed his mind about getting closer to me because I was leaving, but at least I'd *know* what he wanted.

I was a successful woman who usually spoke her mind, but for some reason, I couldn't bear the thought of him rejecting me after I poured my heart out to him.

But was it really better to never take that chance?

"Thanks for making lunch," Kaleb said as he polished off the last of the picnic meal I'd brought with us on our horse ride around his property.

We'd ended up back by the river because I could never resist visiting this picturesque spot, and I'd brought food to feed both of us.

Kaleb was going to actually do some fishing while I read a book I'd been dying to read since its release.

I'd finally ordered it and got it delivered to his place.

*Tell him right now! He's relaxed and upbeat. Talk to him!*

I probably needed those answers.

"It was nothing considering all you've done for me," I said honestly.

I'd baked what my mother used to call picnic pasties with ready-made pastry dough. I'd stuffed them with whatever I found in the pantry and refrigerator and called it lunch.

I'd added some chips to the picnic bag, along with some fruit and a few bottles of beer.

It wasn't exactly gourmet, but Kaleb had torn into the food like he hadn't eaten in weeks.

I'd also brought the blanket that we were currently lounging on after we'd eaten.

The food was cleaned up and the trash was back in the bag.

"It was good," Kaleb commented as he stretched his legs out and took a gulp of the beer I'd just handed him.

"Are you going to fish?" I asked.

He put a hand on his stomach. "In a little while. I'm full. I almost feel too lazy to fish right now. Why? Are you dying to dive into your book?"

I shook my head. "No."

*Oh, for God's sake, just tell him you want to talk!*

I performed in front of sold out stadiums and venues all over the world, and I couldn't tell Kaleb how I felt?

It was getting ridiculous.

And I was past the point that I could keep a rein on my emotions.

I sucked at not having answers, but to have those answers, I needed to talk to Kaleb honestly.

That was the way we'd always been with each other before I'd lost the ability to compartmentalize my emotions when it came to him.

I took a deep breath. "Do you remember all those crazy things I said at The Mug And Jug after I had those sluggers?"

"I remember," he answered in a lazy drawl.

*Keep going, Anna. Keep going.*

"Maybe I don't remember everything, but I wasn't so drunk that I didn't know what I wanted. What I still want," I blurted out. "If I don't explore the way I feel about you, I know I'm going to regret it. I've never felt this way before about any other man, and I don't want to leave without saying how I feel. Maybe you don't feel the same way you did weeks ago. Maybe it would be better if we just let it go. I know I have to leave. God, I don't know, but I feel like I need you to at least know how I'm feeling—"

I hit my back so fast that my head was spinning. Kaleb literally tackled me, controlled my fall, and brought his ripped body down over mine.

"Fuck!" he cursed as he threaded his hands into my hair. "I know we need to talk about this, but I can't wait another second to do this."

His mouth came down on mine with the same desperate urgency I felt every time I looked at him.

Heat flooded between my thighs as I wrapped my arms around his neck and returned the frenzied kiss.

Maybe we did need to talk, but I needed this more.

Kaleb devoured my mouth, and I opened for him, giving him access to anything he wanted.

I'd been burning for this man since the day we'd met, and that fire had been stoked to inferno strength for weeks now.

Weeks of that need for Kaleb all poured out of my body as I clawed at the back of his neck, needing to get closer to him than I'd ever been before.

When he finally raised his head, his eyes were full of wild hunger, and his chest was heaving like he'd just run a marathon.

I was panting as our gazes devoured each other, both of us stunned, but eager to finish what we'd just started.

"Don't ever think that I don't feel the same way you do," Kaleb growled. "I've wanted you naked and in my bed since day one."

God, I'd felt the same way, and the desire to have Kaleb deep inside me was elemental right now.

I wrapped my legs around his hips and surged up just to feel what I wanted so desperately.

His cock was hard and ready to give me exactly what I was craving. I needed Kaleb, and that need was eating me alive.

"I want…" I moaned, my voice trailing off because I couldn't express my longing in words.

Turns out, I didn't need to say the words.

I wanted, and Kaleb responded.

"I know what you want," he rasped against my ear, his breath leaving a trail of warmth on the side of my neck as he nipped at my earlobe. "You want me to make you come. And I want that, too."

He kissed me again, and my body writhed beneath him as he slid his hand beneath my T-shirt and expertly unclasped the front of my bra.

My core clenched so hard it was almost painful as his fingers stroked over one of my breasts until he found my nipple.

I gasped as he pinched it just hard enough to make me moan against his lips.

"Yes!" I hissed as he released my mouth.

My body was on fire for this man, and I needed him inside me.

"Fuck me, Kaleb," I pleaded as his fingers continued to torment my nipples. "I need you."

I'd needed this for what felt like forever, and now that I had him, I couldn't contain those emotions.

"Easy, sweetheart," he crooned low and sexy next to my ear. "I want to touch you. I've wanted to touch you like this for a long time. You're so damn beautiful, Anna."

I shivered as his palm skimmed down my body until he reached the button of my jeans.

*Yes! Touch me! Please touch me!*

At that moment, Kaleb became my entire world, the only thing that existed, and my body was tight with anticipation.

He buried his head against my neck, leaving a trail of heat against my sensitive skin.

This man knew exactly what to do to make me insane, but I relished every second of the sensual torment.

"If you don't fuck me, I think I'm going to lose it," I said with a moan.

"You're going to lose it," he promised in a sensual, wicked voice. "I'm going to make sure that you do. Do you have any idea how much I've wanted to see you come for me, Anna?"

"No," I squeaked as he nipped at my neck.

I didn't know this sensual part of Kaleb, but I was dying to delve into it.

He lowered the zipper on my jeans, and yanked them down enough to give him access to my pussy.

I jerked the second his fingers made contact with my slick heat.

My body was so revved up that the erotic contact was almost too much.

"Kaleb," I whispered his name on a long sigh of satisfaction.

His motions were unhurried, like he wanted to savor the feel of my body.

"Christ!" Kaleb said huskily. "You're so wet. So hot. So fucking perfect."

I whimpered as his fingers found and stroked over my clit. "Kaleb!" I moaned with a lot more urgency.

My hips came up, my body begging for release.

"More," I pleaded right before his mouth covered mine all over again.

He explored my mouth with his tongue with more control and much more leisurely than the first time while I completely lost my mind.

He finally gave me what I needed, stroking harder over my clit until my hips were rocking, my body coiled tight.

When he lifted his head, I let out a desperate sound that I'd never heard come out of my mouth before.

"Oh, my God," I cried out as the coil in my belly started to unfurl.

"Look at me, Anna," Kaleb demanded.

Our eyes met, and I fell into those gorgeous green eyes as my orgasm started to roll over me.

"That's it," Kaleb said in a demanding voice I'd never heard before. "Come for me, Anna."

There was no damn way I could have stopped the powerful orgasm.

I clutched his T-shirt as I threw my head back and moaned helplessly as waves of ecstasy tore through me.

I struggled to catch my breath as Kaleb rolled and held me on top of him protectively.

"Better?" he asked as he kissed the top of my head.

"Not that much better," I said breathlessly. "I really need to get you naked."

He grabbed my wrists as I reached to take off his T-shirt. "Relax, Anna," he said in a husky voice. "My control is hanging by a thread right now, and there's no way I'm going to lose my shit out here. The last thing I want to do is get you completely naked where someone could see you. It might be my land, but there are people who have permission to come here, including my brothers."

"Shit!" I said in a disappointed voice.

I really didn't want his brothers to see me naked, either.

Kaleb wrapped his arms tightly around my body, and I laid my head on his shoulder.

"Then why did you do that?" I asked curiously.

"Because I needed to at least touch you," he answered, his voice graveled and raw.

I could hear the edginess in his tone, but his touch was gentle as he stroked his hand up and down my back in a comforting motion.

I ached to touch him, give him the same pleasure he'd given me, but I squashed that desire for now.

I was intimately close to him, and that was enough for now.

"Thank you," I said softly.

"For giving you an orgasm," he teased.

"No. For always trying to protect me."

Kaleb was probably the most selfless guy I'd ever known.

He always had my back, and I trusted him completely.

That was what made our relationship so special.

"That's an instinct I'll never be able to ease up on, Anna. You'll have to get used to it."

I smiled.

I was already used to it, and having someone who cared enough about me to watch out for me and my best interests was addictive.

I silently hoped I'd never have to see what it was like to be without Kaleb Remington watching my back.

## Chapter 21

*Kaleb*

"Yo! Kaleb! Did you hear a word that I just said?" Tanner asked as we sat in my home office later that evening.

"I heard you," I lied. "I'm fine with going ahead with the acquisition if Devon is on board, too."

I vaguely knew what he was talking about, and I knew he wanted this company.

I didn't need to hear all the details, but I trusted Tanner's judgment.

*Fuck!* It wasn't like me not to have all of my focus on a pending project, but after what had happened at the river earlier with Anna, I was distracted.

"You didn't hear a word I said," Tanner accused. "I didn't ask for your permission. I asked for your input on how to go about the acquisition. Where is your head tonight?"

I ran a frustrated hand through my hair. "I'm sorry. I guess I'm off my game today."

Tanner smirked. "Does that have anything to do with the beautiful woman in your music room who's discussing her awards show performance via a virtual meeting?"

"It's Sunday for fuck's sake," I told him, irritated. "You would think they could wait until tomorrow."

The only reason I'd agreed to discuss this project with Tanner tonight is because I knew that Anna would be tied up in a meeting. Otherwise, I would have told him to go screw himself until we go into the office tomorrow.

"You're really uptight," Tanner observed.

Hell, yes, I was irritated.

I'd waited all damn day to get Anna alone at home, and we were sitting in two separate rooms going over business on a Sunday.

A few months ago, this would have been a normal occurrence. I'd worked every single day. But I hadn't even looked at a business document on the weekends since Anna had come to stay with me, and now I liked it that way.

"We'll deal with this tomorrow," Tanner said sympathetically. "Are you okay?"

"I'm fine," I said dismissively. "I just don't feel like dealing with business on the weekend."

Tanner raised a brow from his chair across the desk from me. "Who are you, and what did you do with my workaholic older brother?"

"I told you that I was evaluating my priorities. If you must know, I'm trying to figure out how I'm going to convince Anna that we need to see each other after she leaves for California."

That very issue had been on my mind all day.

There was no way in hell that I could take her to bed and casually say goodbye to her in two weeks' time.

That was not going to work for me.

*Not. Going. To. Happen.*

"I'm glad you finally figured out that you need her. I've never seen you live a somewhat balanced life, and you haven't had a single nightmare about Shelby since you met Anna. I think *she* was that priority that was completely missing from your life, Kaleb. You needed a reason to live a more balanced life," Tanner said, his voice relieved. "You'll work it out. If you care about her, there's no reason why you can't see each other. It might be complicated, but I think she's worth it. I don't think it will take much convincing. She's crazy about you, too. She's going to want to see you. It's not like you can't work remote if you want to stay in California for a while. Devon and I are both in the office most of the time."

"I'll talk to her about it later," I told him. "What are you doing here anyway? Isn't Lauren coming home soon? How is she doing?"

Lauren Collier was extremely close to Tanner. In fact, she was almost like an honorary little sister to him. He'd been watching out for her since her brother, Keith, had died. Keith Collier had been Tanner's best friend, and when he'd died suddenly just when Lauren had been leaving for college, Tanner had made it his business to take care of her. Keith had been Lauren's guardian, and she'd had no other family.

"Still as smart as ever," Tanner said with a grin. "She'll be staying with me for a few weeks. She's coming home permanently. She's tired of living on the East Coast and she has enough experience to move back to Montana now and work remotely. She wants to find a place of her own before she makes that move."

Lauren had a PhD in economics, and she'd been working as a market researcher for the last few years on the East Coast.

I liked Lauren. Always had. She was gifted, and she'd flown through her PhD in record time. I'd also known her most of her life, and she'd become like a member of our family over the years.

"I'm sure you're happy," I commented.

Even though Lauren had a doctorate and was all grown up, I knew that Tanner still worried about her long distance.

He nodded. "I am happy. She'll be arriving in a day or two. It's been too long since I've seen her in person."

I hadn't seen her for a while. Tanner had flown for brief visits with her in Boston, but she hadn't been back to Montana for a few years. "Bring her over," I suggested. "I'd like to see her, too."

"I'd like to," Tanner said hesitantly. "But there might be a problem with that. She's a huge Annelise fan."

"You really think she'd recognize her? No one else has," I reminded him.

He shrugged. "Maybe not. I guess we can deal with that if it happens. Lauren would never tell anyone if she knew it was a secret. I trust her. Did you tell Anna about the shell company?"

"Yeah," I answered. "She took it pretty well considering she lost a few million dollars. She wasn't that concerned about losing the money. She's more worried about the fact that it was an unusual investment for her father. I think she suspects the same thing we do. That it could be connected to her parents' murders."

"It's honestly the only thing that makes sense since her mom and dad really had no enemies," Tanner said thoughtfully.

"I'm not that comfortable with Anna coming out of hiding for this awards performance," I told Tanner truthfully. "What if she becomes the new target? It's going to become very obvious that she knows the truth soon. That shell company has been cut off from receiving any more money from her."

The thought of Anna being in any kind of danger made me even more uptight.

"That might be unlikely," Tanner replied. "Now that the feds are onto them, I'd think they'd be too busy trying to avoid prosecution to pursue some kind of revenge. Honestly, is it even possible for anyone to get to Annelise Kendrick? She'd be a hell of a lot harder to get access to than her parents."

I nodded. "She has good security at her place in Beverly Hills, and she usually has bodyguards close by for events and appearances. The security will be especially tight for this awards performance. But I still don't like it. There could be someone out there who wants to hurt her, Tanner," I grumbled.

"You do realize that you're going to have to get used to the fact that you'll have to share her with the rest of the world, right?" Tanner questioned.

"I'll share Annelise because I have to do it," I said, disgruntled. "Anna is a different story."

Logically, I knew those two women were the same person, but I hadn't really seen that much of Annelise in the Anna I'd gotten to know and care about. Nothing was familiar to me when it came to her public personality except her music.

The music room had been soundproofed, but I'd listened to her play many times.

Sometimes it was a song she'd written that she wanted me to hear, but she still enjoyed playing classical music, too, and luckily, she usually asked me to sit with her when she felt like playing classical.

Annelise was a brand that had been carefully created.

Anna was real, and I was willing to do almost anything to make sure the woman I cared about stayed safe.

"We have two weeks," Tanner reminded me. "The feds might make some progress before she leaves for California. Enjoy the time you have with Anna right now and stop thinking about what's going to happen when she's back in California. We have a security team that we almost never use ourselves."

"Don't think that I haven't thought about putting them on her gorgeous ass every minute of the day when she's back in California," I said in an agitated tone.

"I'm not sure she'd go for that," Tanner said doubtfully. "Her life is already stifled enough in her world."

"Fuck! I know that. I don't want to strangle her. I just want her to be safe. They could tail her without getting in her way."

Tanner shot me a concerned glance. "You do realize she's thirty-five years old and she's lived with all of this her entire adult life, right?"

"That was before we met," I said unhappily. "And before her parents were murdered. I know that she's generally cautious, and I trust her judgment, but I don't have a good feeling about any of this."

"You have the best instincts I've ever seen, in and out of business," Tanner said solemnly. "Trust them."

The problem was that I wasn't sure if they were my true instincts anymore or if I was just paranoid about something happening to Anna.

For the first time in my life, I wasn't sure if I could trust my gut because my judgment was skewed when it came to Anna.

Tanner rose from his chair to leave, and I walked him out to the front door.

"I'll probably be coming in late to the office tomorrow," I told him distractedly as I opened the front door. "I'm hoping Anna and I can talk later."

Tanner sent me an irritated look. "We have an entire team that does most of the work once we make a decision, Kaleb. You have two weeks with Anna. Come in when you feel like it. Or don't come in at all. We've worked our asses off for years now to get to where we are right now. This is the time when we should start enjoying the benefits of giving up our personal lives for all those years. I won't be coming into the office for at least a day or two when Lauren gets here to look for a place, and I'll be leaving early after that until she goes back to Boston. I haven't spent any quality time with her for years."

He was right, but old habits were hard to break. I'd spent my entire adult life hyper focused on KTD.

I gravitated toward the music room after Tanner left. The door was partially open, so I could tell that Anna was having a lively conversation with someone about the upcoming awards show.

Eventually, I wandered out to the barn and worked a little on a table in the heated woodworking shop that I'd never used before I'd met Anna.

Tanner was right. I *was* going to have to learn to share the woman I cared about with the world.

It was unreasonable to think that she'd ever have a normal life.

Hell, I didn't always live a normal life, either.

Annelise was part of Anna, and she worked long hours on her music sometimes.

I could live with that as long as she was in my life.

There would be times when I'd be consumed with work, too.

Shit happened.

Deals had to be troubleshooted sometimes when they were in danger of falling through.

I worked for nearly an hour on the table that I was making for Anna to put in the music room.

I was determined that my home was going to become a second home for her, a place for her to come back to whenever she needed some peace.

I ran my hand over the surface I'd just sanded down. I realized that my life was going to be extremely complicated now that Anna was a huge part of it.

I grinned as I put my woodworking tools away.

In a short period of time, Anna Kendrick had turned my very controlled world upside down.

Maybe I'd avoided complicated relationships in the past, but now, I was actually looking forward to it.

## Chapter 22

*Anna*

I t was well after one in the morning by the time I exited the
music room.

It had been a marathon meeting because I'd wanted to wrap up
all of the details with the awards show so I could spend as much time
with Kaleb as possible before I had to leave.

I was doing a familiar routine for the performance, one I could
almost do in my sleep because I'd performed the same number over
and over again while I was on tour.

However, there had still been a lot of details to go over with the
organizers to make sure everything would be set up like I needed
it to be.

I stretched my back out before I wandered the lower level of the
house, looking to see if Kaleb was still awake.

Most likely, he wasn't.

Tomorrow was Monday, and he had to get up early.

When I didn't see or hear him in any of the rooms, I figured he'd
headed upstairs.

I would have done the same.

I'd went into the meeting hours ago, and he'd had no idea when I'd be surfacing again.

I turned off the lights downstairs and headed up to my room, noticing that Kaleb's bedroom door was closed and there was no illumination coming from under the door as I passed his bedroom.

My heart ached as I realized I had missed the opportunity to spend the evening with him.

Yeah, my marathon meeting had been necessary, but I was still disappointed.

After our interlude at the river today, I was extremely restless.

We'd discussed sex openly for the first time, and I'd let him know that I hadn't been with anyone for a long time, but that I was on birth control and clean of any sexual diseases.

He'd told me the same thing.

That sex talk that most intimate couples had was a lot more natural than it had ever been previously for me.

Maybe because he was also my friend, and we could say almost anything to each other.

Eventually, Kaleb had fished for a while, and I'd tried to read my book, but my mind kept wandering to more carnal places, and all I'd really done was watch...*him.*

We'd had a quick dinner when we'd arrived back at the house, and we hadn't really had a chance to talk or communicate that much before my meeting.

Our relationship had been forever changed after that intimate moment at the river earlier, and I couldn't say that I was sorry about that.

The uncertainty between the two of us had morphed into something entirely different.

Now, the constant awareness of his presence and the physical ache of knowing that we wanted each other the same way was nearly killing me.

It was a relief that we weren't dancing around our feelings anymore, but now that I knew he definitely felt the same way, I wanted to be as close to him as possible.

I changed into my pajamas, and looked at my empty bed.

For the first time since I'd arrived, it looked cold and lonely.

*Nope!*

That wasn't going to be enough for me tonight.

It wasn't the need to get him naked that drew me to his bedroom door.

I just wanted to be close to him, and feel his warm and welcoming body next to me.

Now that I knew that I was welcome in his bed, I had to be close to him as often as possible because there would be nights in the future that I'd have to be alone again.

I didn't want to waste any of the time we had left together.

I opened the door slowly, trying not to wake him, and closed it behind me.

I'd seen his bedroom suite, but I didn't know it as well as my own.

Luckily, there was enough light coming from his windows to find my way to his bed.

There wasn't enough natural light to see his face clearly from a distance, but I recognized that muscular body and bare chest as I slid into his bed.

I moved closer to his warmth carefully, finally content to be sharing the same space with him.

As usual, he warmed up the bed with his body heat, and I luxuriated in the feeling of being next to him again.

I'd slept better than I'd ever slept before when I'd spent those nights in bed with him at the cabin.

I closed my eyes when I'd gotten as close to him as possible without waking him, feeling like I was exactly where I belonged.

"It's about damn time that you brought your gorgeous ass to my bed," Kaleb said huskily in a voice that sounded very…awake.

"You're not sleeping," I said as my eyes popped open again.

He wrapped an arm around my waist and pulled me against his hard body.

"Hell, no, I'm not sleeping. I was waiting for you. I was going to come and get you if I didn't see you in the next few minutes. I heard you come upstairs. Obviously, you finally finished that meeting."

"Yes," I informed him as I cuddled as closely to his body as I could get. "I'm sorry. It ran way longer than I'd anticipated, but I doubt I'll have to do much more than touch base with them if they have any further issues before the ceremony. I can't believe you're still awake. It's after one. I just…wanted to be close to you. I wasn't planning on waking you up."

"You didn't," he grumbled. "I missed you, and there's no way in hell you'll ever sleep alone again in this house."

I released a long, relieved breath.

He wanted to be with me as much as I wanted to be with him, and that made me happier than I'd been for a very long time.

I wrapped my arms around his neck and savored the feel of his large, ripped body against mine. "You should be asleep. It's late."

He rolled me onto my back, and covered my body with his. "Do you really think I give a rat's ass what time it is? You're here. In my fucking bed. And I can finally touch you. Do you have any idea how torturous it was for me to sleep in the same bed at the cabin? It nearly killed me not to touch you, woman. But we need to get a few things straight."

God, I'd felt the same way at the cabin, but now that I knew Kaleb, it was so much more difficult not to touch him.

My emotions were everywhere, and I wasn't capable of compartmentalizing those feelings like I'd done at the cabin anymore.

"Like?" I prompted.

"Like the fact that I have to let you go back to California because your work life is there, but you'll have to accept that I'm going to worry, and I'm going to try to protect you. We're also going to see each other as much as possible. I'll come to California, and you can come here whenever you can break free. Once you've spent the night in my bed, you're also going to have to deal with being *mine*. I've discovered that I'm a greedy bastard when it comes to you, and I won't share. As long as we're together, there's only going to be you for me, Anna. I have to know that there's only going to be me for you, too."

My heart tripped at his words.

He wanted an exclusive relationship, and I was so elated that I almost wanted to cry.

I could never share him, either.

Seriously, like there could ever be another guy for me when I had exactly what I wanted and needed with Kaleb Remington?

"I'm going to be thirty-six years old this year, Kaleb," I informed him, my heart beating erratically. "I've never wanted a man the way I want you. Do you really think any other guy would exist for me when I'm with you?"

"Good," he said in an impatient voice. "Now that we've gotten those conditions straight, I'm about done with this conversation. I've waited way too fucking long to be in this position, and I don't want to waste the time that I still have to be with you."

I actually giggled as he sat up with me and started to peel off my sleep shirt.

That was so Kaleb. He'd been direct and succinct, and then the entire conversation was over with and done pretty quickly.

I was onboard with that.

For now, Kaleb Remington was mine, and I didn't want to waste time talking about something we didn't really need to hash out.

Right now, all I wanted to do was feel Kaleb.

I desperately needed to be skin-to-skin with his enormous body.

I helped him shed my pajamas and panties as quickly as possible, and then let out a startled gasp as he pulled me into him again and realized he was already completely naked.

Bliss rolled over my entire body as our bodies met with nothing between the two of us.

"I sleep in the raw sometimes because I sleep hot," he mentioned in a low, sexy drawl right next to my ear.

He'd always slept in sweatpants at the cabin, but he'd obviously done that for me.

"I have absolutely no issue with that," I squeaked as he nipped my earlobe.

"Relax, sweetheart," he told me as he lowered our upper bodies to the bed without breaking our skin-to-skin contact. "You feel tense, and not in a good way."

"I think…" I said breathlessly. "I think I'm as nervous as a virgin, and I'm definitely not a virgin. It's just been a long time for me."

My emotions were running rampant, and I felt as raw and as vulnerable as I'd ever felt before.

"How long?" he asked in a calming tone.

"Eight years," I blurted out. "I told you that I'd stopped looking for Mr. Right. I didn't want to have sex with anyone just to get laid. I can give myself an orgasm if I need one."

"Fuck! I'd like to see that someday," he said in a low, aroused voice. "Do you trust me, Anna?"

"You know I do," I told him earnestly. "But I'm not all that sexually experienced. I know that might be a little surprising to you. I am Annelise, and she radiates sexuality. I—"

"Stop!" Kaleb said gruffly. "I don't want Annelise in my bed. I just want…you."

And then he kissed me, an embrace that was so possessive and carnal that I forgot all about the fact that I hadn't been with very many guys in my life.

For me, in that moment, the only man who existed was Kaleb.

## Chapter 23

*Anna*

"Kaleb," I murmured fervently as he released my mouth. "I want to touch you. Please."

I wanted to get to know his body intimately just like he'd become acquainted with mine earlier.

I pushed against his shoulders, and he let me roll him onto his back.

If he hadn't consented, there was no way I'd be able to shove a guy with his size and muscle off me easily.

My mouth was immediately all over his warm skin, exploring his chest, his six-pack abs, and that beautifully formed V pattern that pointed directly to the place I wanted to go.

I wasn't great at oral sex, but I didn't give a shit about my inexperience anymore.

I was eager to please him like he'd done with me earlier, and I wanted to put my own brand on every part of his body.

I wanted him in my mouth so I could explore him like he'd explored my body earlier.

I trailed my hand down his body, and wrapped my hand around his very large cock.

"Fuck!" Kaleb groaned as my fingers explored the velvety surface. He felt so damn good, so hard, but so silky smooth on the surface.

I lowered my head and tasted his cock, savoring the slightly salty bead of moisture that was at the very tip slowly and thoroughly.

I moaned as I took him deeper, suddenly greedy for more of him.

"You're killing me right now, Anna," Kaleb warned, his voice tight with barely leashed control.

I'd never heard that note of desperation in his voice, and it sent an excited chill down my spine.

I wanted him to want me.

I wanted him to need me.

And I really wanted to taste that frantic desire when he came in my mouth.

I wrapped my fingers a little tighter around the root of his cock and sucked in as much of him as I could possibly take, applying as much suction as possible as I pulled back again.

He threaded his fingers into my hair and guided me, showing me exactly what he needed.

I got lost in that erotic rhythm, savoring every harsh, guttural sound that came from his throat as I sucked him exactly the way he wanted.

I was startled when I was suddenly jerked away from his cock, and landed on my back on the bed.

"One more second of that, and I'll be coming in that beautiful mouth of yours," Kaleb said harshly from above me. "Jesus, Anna! You make me completely insane."

I wrapped my arms around his neck as I used a sultry voice that had never come out of my mouth before. "I *wanted* you to come in my mouth. I wanted to taste you, Kaleb."

"Not this time," he rasped as he buried his face in my neck and moved his mouth over my sensitive skin. "I need to bury my cock inside that gorgeous body of yours, Anna. I want to take what's mine."

"Yes," I said breathily as I raised my hips, needing exactly the same thing. "Fuck me, Kaleb."

I wanted to be taken just as much as he wanted to take me.

I wanted our bodies intimately connected.

It was something I'd wanted for so long that I was frantic to have him inside me.

I clawed at his back as he slid his hand slowly down my body until he reached my wet pussy.

"Tell me you want me, Anna," he demanded. "Tell me what you need."

I gasped as he slid his fingers into my heat.

God, he already knew what I needed.

I was so wet that his fingers were coated in that moisture the moment he touched my pussy.

"Kaleb," I whimpered, my voice tormented with need. "You know I do."

"Tell. Me," he said in a husky, bossy voice that I'd never heard when he was talking to me.

That commanding tone of his wrung the words from my lips immediately. "I need you. I need your cock inside of me right now. I need you to make me come before I lose my mind."

I had to be closer to him than we'd ever been before, and I needed it right this second.

"I'd like to take this slow. I want to taste that gorgeous pussy of yours, but that's going to have to wait," he growled as he moved his hand and shifted his massive body between my thighs.

My hands moved down his back until they landed on his tight ass. "No more waiting, Kaleb. No more teasing. I can't take anymore. Fuck me."

One powerful surge and he was balls deep inside me.

A loud moan of satisfaction left my lips as my fingernails dug into his skin.

He was a big man, and it had been a long time for me.

Kaleb stretched me, but that small discomfort didn't even faze me.

I was finally intimately connected to this man, and I never wanted to be separated from him again.

I wrapped my legs around his waist and surged up with every thrust, meeting his fierce movements with my own.

I got utterly lost in the sensation, in the rhythm, and in this man who was like no other that had ever touched me before.

He put his hands under my ass, pulling me up to grind against him every time he buried his cock inside me.

"Oh, God, Kaleb, you feel so good," I told him, panting.

Perspiration dotted our skin as our bodies moved together, both of us reaching for more.

I couldn't get enough of Kaleb to satisfy me.

"You're fucking mine, Anna. Say it!" Kaleb demanded harshly.

"I'll always be yours," I said breathlessly as my palms slid up the sweat slickened skin of his back and into his coarse hair. "And you'll always be mine."

The powerful connection and chemistry I'd always had with Kaleb felt like it suddenly clicked into place.

I wanted to claim him as much as he wanted to claim me.

It was always supposed to be this way, but we'd fought it tooth and nail in the beginning.

I closed my eyes, and my head fell back as I felt my orgasm start to unfurl in my belly.

It was a powerful sensation, and wholly unfamiliar to me.

I was about to climax harder than I ever had before, and I didn't shy away from it, even though it was a little bit scary.

"Let it go, Anna," he rasped near my ear as he ground down hard, stimulating my clit to the point of madness. "Let it go."

I had no idea how he knew that I was close to orgasm, but we were so connected right now that I didn't even try to figure it out.

I wrapped my legs tighter around his waist and ground against him hard as he sped up to a frenzied pace.

"Yes!" I moaned loudly with abandon. "Kaleb!"

No other words would leave my lips as my core clenched in spasms around his cock that were almost painful.

I grabbed his shoulders, and then clawed at his back, holding on for dear life.

"Fuck!" Kaleb groaned as he fucked me harder, trying to draw out my climax as long as possible.

Pure euphoria that made my body thrum rolled over me as Kaleb buried himself deep inside me and found his own release.

Both of us stilled for a moment, and the bedroom was quiet except for the sound of our labored breathing as we recovered.

Kaleb rolled and pulled me on top of him to protect me from getting squished beneath his larger form.

He ran his fingertips over my back in a soothing motion that made me sigh with gratification.

"Okay," I said a few moments later, still in awe of what had just happened. "So that's what it's like to have really mind-blowing sex. I think I'm completely addicted."

He slapped my bare ass playfully. "You better be," he said in a lazy baritone. "I already told you that I won't share."

"There isn't a woman on the planet who would want anyone else after *that*," I teased. "You're stuck with me, Kaleb Remington. Maybe I do stupid things sometimes, like trudging through a major blizzard and breaking into a house to survive, but I'm not a total idiot."

"You're one of the most intelligent women I've ever known," Kaleb shared as he tightened his arms around my waist. "And you're definitely the most creative person I've ever met."

"But I'll never be a financial genius like you are," I reminded him.

"You don't need to be," he said with a chuckle. "You've got me."

Some people might think that comment was a little arrogant, but I knew it wasn't meant to be.

Kaleb was simply stating a fact and letting me know that he cared enough about me to always be there for me. He was also saying that I didn't have to be perfect because he himself didn't think he was talented with much else except numbers and acquisitions.

He'd probably never recognize how special he was, but he didn't need to. *He* had *me* to remind him of that.

Who would have ever imagined that an Ivy League billionaire and a pop star with no college education would end up being this happy together?

If I wasn't living it, I probably wouldn't have believed it myself.

We should have absolutely nothing in common, but the two of us just fit like two pieces of a jigsaw puzzle that went together perfectly.

We may not always agree about everything, but most couples had plenty of disagreements.

Would I have connected with Kaleb if I'd met the business mogul part of him first?

Yeah.

Probably.

I found it hard to believe that I wouldn't have seen right through that alpha, business genius exterior and into his huge heart.

"I think I need a shower," I said.

Unfortunately, I'd have to get up from my comfortable spot on top of Kaleb to get there.

"Is that an invitation, beautiful?" he asked huskily.

I hadn't meant that statement to be provocative, but…

"I think it could be," I said playfully.

I squealed happily as he sat up and took me with him as he stood.

I wrapped my legs around his waist as he cupped my ass and walked toward the bathroom.

"Kaleb, it's late. You have to work tomorrow," I reminded him.

He turned on the light in the bathroom and grinned down at me. "I've evaluated my priorities, and you're at the very top of that list. I'll go to the office late if I decide to go at all."

My heart skipped a beat as I looked at his determined expression.

My goal was, after all, to make sure he didn't go back to his workaholic ways, and the man had never looked happier than he did right now.

"In that case," I answered in a teasing tone. "Let's take a very long shower."

"That's the plan, sweetheart," he said in a wicked voice I was starting to adore.

He threaded his hands into my hair and pulled my mouth to his for a very thorough, satisfying embrace that left me breathless before he even turned on the water.

# Chapter 24

*Kaleb*

"**M**om has decided that she's doing a last-minute barbecue as a goodbye party for Anna," Tanner informed me a week later as my brothers and I sat in my office in Billings.

"She's not leaving forever," I said grumpily.

"You'll see her more often than we do," Devon said stubbornly. "You're going to the awards ceremony, so you'll see her not long after she leaves. She might not come back to Montana for a while. I think it's a great idea. She can see everyone she's going to miss all at one time, including me."

I sent my youngest brother an annoyed look, but I didn't bother to address his ridiculous comment.

I'd eagerly accepted when Anna had asked me to be her date for the awards ceremony. It was a big moment for her because she was nominated for several awards, and I wouldn't miss it. She'd have to slip away for her performance, but I'd be by her side most of the night.

"You do know that once you're seen with Anna as her date, your life will never be the same," Tanner cautioned.

I grinned. "My life hasn't been the same since the moment we met. And yes, I realize it will shove me into a hornet's nest of speculation and gossip, but I'm not going to hide my relationship with Anna. I'm proud of her. I support her. And I don't give a shit if everyone knows that."

I didn't want to hide the fact that Anna and I were together.

There was actually a very large part of me that wanted to be seen with her so every asshole in California knew that she was already taken.

Yeah, I liked my privacy, but I liked Anna a hell of a lot more.

We'd spent the last week making up for lost time in my bed.

And all around the entire house.

I couldn't keep my damn hands off her when she was within touching distance.

I had no idea how this was going to work when we lived in different states, but Tanner had been right when he'd said I could make this relationship happen.

I could be with Anna in two hours or so in my jet.

Or I could send my jet to bring her to me when she could break free.

No, it wasn't ideal.

But it was a lot better than saying goodbye to her and never seeing her at all.

"I'm seriously going to miss her," Devon said earnestly.

"Me, too," Tanner added solemnly.

I knew my mother was going to miss seeing Anna almost every day, too.

The two of them had gotten close in the weeks that Anna had been here.

"She's not gone yet," I said irritably. "When is this barbecue happening? Mom hasn't said a word about it to me."

I still had one more week before I had to think about what it was like without her living with me every single day, and I planned on pushing those negative thoughts off as long as possible.

The last week had been the best one of my life, and I wasn't going to moon over how lonely it would be without her when she was still here.

"Mom probably hasn't had a chance to mention it to you because you and Anna have barely surfaced in the last week," Devon said wryly.

He was right. I'd talked to my mother on the phone, but I hadn't seen her in well over a week.

"The barbecue is Sunday," Tanner informed me. "Anna said she's leaving next Monday because she has rehearsals that week before the ceremony. Don't worry. It's early in the afternoon. You'll have that evening together before she goes."

It was Monday, so we had a week before Anna boarded my jet to fly back to California.

She'd argued about using my jet, but I'd convinced her that it was the simplest way for her to get back to Los Angeles.

I wasn't going anywhere, so there was no reason for her to hire a damn charter that may or may not be in good mechanical shape.

I finally nodded. "I'm sure Anna will appreciate Mom's thoughtfulness."

Maybe it was better if Anna could say goodbye to everyone at the same time.

It would save her from having to run around town and see everyone before she left.

Hell, I knew I was selfish, but I wanted to spend as much time with her as I could get.

I had come into the office during the last week, but usually only when I knew that Anna would be tied up with obligations or virtual meetings.

She'd had a few calls today, one of them an additional meeting with the feds that they'd requested.

I was hopeful that they might tell her something about the investigation.

She'd already given them all of the information she possibly could on that shell company.

It would be great if the feds were more forthcoming than the police department in California. If they knew anything, they still weren't talking. Logically, them not sharing information during the investigation made sense. Their job was to work for the victims to get justice for them. Releasing any information to anyone during that investigation was a decidedly bad idea.

However, I also knew how much Anna desperately needed answers, and I wanted her to get those answers. The waiting without any resolution in sight was hell on the family left behind.

"I'll swing by to see Mom when I get back to Crystal Fork," I told my brothers. "I'll ask if there's anything she needs help with for the party."

"I think she'd rather you didn't," Devon said jokingly. "She's pretty happy that you two are spending all of your free time together and not coming up for air."

I looked at Tanner.

He nodded. "He's right. I think she's already planning your wedding for you, and counting the grandchildren she'll finally get. Since Devon and I are apparently hopeless, she has all her hopes pinned on you and Anna at the moment."

"How in the hell did she find out that we're more than just friends?" I asked in an annoyed voice.

I hadn't even told my mother that Anna and I were dating yet.

Tanner and Devon put their hands in the air. "Hey, don't look at us," Devon said innocently. "I think she got the whole idea into her head because she hasn't seen Anna, either, in the last week. It doesn't take a genius to figure out that you two are crazy about each other and spending all your free time together. Tanner and I knew almost immediately. If you're not coming into the office, you're with Anna. Nothing else could drag you away from this place."

I didn't bother to deny that I was crazy about Anna. It was true, and I wasn't going to hide how I felt about her anymore.

She was a very important part of my life now, and I didn't give a shit who knew that.

"Just don't encourage her," I warned Devon. "I have no idea how this will all work out in the end. It's going to be complicated."

"You'll both make it work," Tanner said firmly. "It's weird because you haven't even known each other that long, but I can't imagine the two of you without each other anymore."

Hell, I couldn't imagine that scenario either, but Anna might get tired of having a man who wasn't always present in her life.

And I literally hated the fact that I might not always be there when she needed me.

"Anna has survived thirty-five years without a serious man in her life," Tanner said thoughtfully. "She'll be fine, Kaleb. She's not the same mentally exhausted and grieving woman who you met at the cabin. She has her shit together. She's writing music. She's dealing with her old life again. She needed a break, and you gave that to her. Anna seems rejuvenated and ready to take her life back again. We all know that the grieving process takes a long time, but she seems happy, and so do you. Don't overthink this situation. Take it one day at a time."

"I was thinking the same thing," Devon said in a serious tone. "I think Anna falling through that window was a gift for both of you. You were there when she needed you, Kaleb. But I think you needed her, too. I think you were as mentally burned out as she was when you met. I'm not seeing that anymore."

"I was still blaming myself for what happened to Shelby, and questioning all of my priorities," I confessed.

"You over all that?" Tanner asked.

I shrugged. "As much as I can be. Shelby's happy and healthy. If her past is in the rearview mirror for her, it was kind of ridiculous for me to dwell on something I can't change. I learned something from that experience, but I'd rather not do it again."

"All Shelby wants is for you to be happy. For all of us to be as happy as she is right now with Wyatt," Devon said. "Although I'm not sure anyone can be as happy as she is with Wyatt. It's almost a little nauseating."

I raised a brow as I looked at my younger brother. "Is there a little bit of envy in there somewhere?"

Devon shook his head adamantly. "Oh, fuck, no! I can't imagine ever being so close to a woman that I can't live without her. I don't think it's in me to feel that way. I think it would be suffocating. It's fine for Shelby, but no thanks. I like my freedom to do whatever I want."

Tanner shot Devon an exasperated look. "We'll remind you of that when some woman knocks you on your ass."

"Never going to happen," Devon said confidently.

Devon liked women of all ages, shapes, and sizes. He could charm a woman easily, but he'd gotten hurt when he was young, and he hadn't taken a relationship seriously since.

I doubted that he was pining over that female after all of these years, but the experience had made him throw up walls that I wasn't sure any woman could manage to scale.

On the surface, Devon could be annoying, but his cynicism hid a very huge heart that was underneath all of that bravado.

"Never say never," Tanner warned him. "Then you never have to regret saying it later."

"I'll never regret saying it," Devon argued. "There's some men who just aren't cut out for a serious relationship that cuts their balls off. That would be me. It's going to have to be you and Kaleb who gives Mom her grandchildren. I'm never getting married."

Tanner glared at Devon. "Don't count on me. I'm not any fonder of serious relationships than you are."

"But you wanted one once," Devon said in a more serious tone.

"At one time, maybe I did," Tanner snapped. "That's water under the bridge, and it doesn't mean I want one now."

If any of us were meant to settle down, it was Tanner.

He'd always wanted kids and a family.

He'd been faithful to the same woman for many years, and he would have bent over backwards for the woman he'd loved.

In fact, he'd always seemed settled, until he wasn't.

I was grateful that he hadn't married the woman who had eventually dumped him, but I hated the fact that it had hurt him for so long after it was over.

"I'm starving. Do you want to grab lunch?" Devon asked in a remorseful tone.

He was obviously sorry that he'd mentioned the whole subject of Tanner getting married and having kids.

"I'm good," I told my brothers as they got up to go find lunch. "I'll probably take off soon. Anna should be done with her calls by early afternoon."

Tanner shot me a knowing look. "I assume that we might not see you until Sunday."

"Maybe not," I informed him. "But I cleared any work that I had to get done earlier. I don't have anything active right now."

I'd planned it that way. I wasn't taking on any new acquisitions until after Anna was gone.

Tanner nodded as he said simply, "That's good. We'd prefer it if we didn't see you until Sunday, and I guarantee Mom will be ecstatic."

He shot me a rare grin before he followed Devon out the door and closed it behind him.

# Chapter 25

*Anna*

I tossed my book aside and reached for the thermos of coffee I'd brought with me down to the river.

I'd finished my phone meetings early, and it had been way too nice of a day to eat lunch inside.

My first thought had been to come here to the river, so I'd ridden down here with Bella to enjoy some time outdoors.

I was free to roam wherever I wanted for another week, and I didn't want to waste a moment of that freedom.

After pouring some coffee into my mug, I took a deep breath and just absorbed the serenity of this particular location.

The mesmerizing sound of the river nearly put me into a daze.

I was tired because I wasn't getting much sleep, but I wasn't about to complain about Kaleb's voracious sexual appetite because I always wanted him as much as he wanted me.

It had been a magical week for me, and it wasn't all about the sex.

Kaleb and I were close in a very different way. We were still friends, but our relationship had shifted now that we were lovers, too.

The intimacy I'd craved for so long was a reality, and it was better than I'd ever imagined it could be.

I was totally open and vulnerable with Kaleb in ways that I hadn't been before, and it satisfied the painful ache I'd experienced every time I'd looked at him in the past.

I was at peace with myself and the world, although it would take me a long time to get past missing my parents horribly. In some ways, I might never get over losing them, but I knew I'd be able to move on with my life even if that pain never completely went away.

I wished I could find a little bit of closure about their murders, but the investigation was still ongoing.

I wanted to know who had killed my parents and why it had happened. It was going to be difficult if it stayed a mystery forever.

I wanted to get justice for my parents. It wouldn't bring them back to me, but I'd feel like someone was being held responsible for what they'd done to my mom and dad.

This morning, I'd been hopeful that the feds would give me some information about the shell company on our call, but they'd only wanted a phone interview to discuss some of the people in my parents' lives.

There was no resolution there, either, but I got the feeling they might be making some kind of headway if they were asking for more personal information about my parents.

"Excuse me," a female voice said quietly from behind me. "I don't want to interrupt, but would you mind if I joined you?"

Startled by hearing another voice in this particular spot, I turned my head to look at the woman who had politely asked to join me.

My eyes went to the horse that was grazing beside Bella.

I'd been so lost in thought that I'd never heard this woman approach on horseback.

Even though Kaleb had told me that other people had permission to use the river property, I'd never seen anyone here before.

I nodded, curious to find out who she was and why she was here. "Sit," I encouraged her as I moved to the side of the blanket I'd brought with me.

*B. A. Scott*

"I'm Lauren Collier," she said as she sat with what I assumed was her lunch and put her hand out. "I love it here, and Kaleb lets me come whenever I'm around."

I shook it, bemused, not recognizing the name.

I didn't recall Kaleb ever mentioning her name before.

"You've never heard about me," she said apologetically. "I can't say I'm surprised. I'm usually pretty forgettable. I'm staying with Tanner for a few weeks."

She was pretty in an understated way, with dark blonde hair that was in a thick braid, and gorgeous blue eyes that were well hidden by a pair of glasses.

Oh, God, could this be the female that had broken Tanner's heart?

Kaleb had mentioned that he'd pointed that woman out at The Mug And Jug the night I'd stupidly downed those sluggers, but I didn't remember it…or the woman I'd seen that night.

Even though she had been polite, I suddenly wanted to punch her in the face.

"You're staying…with Tanner?" I asked cautiously.

"Not staying with him like that," she said, flustered. "I mean, we're not sleeping together. We've never slept together. He's kind of like an overprotective older brother, but we're not related. I've known Tanner all my life. He was my brother's best friend. After my brother Keith died, Tanner unofficially adopted me because my brother was my guardian."

Okay, this definitely wasn't the woman who had broken Tanner's heart. "I'm sorry about your brother," I said automatically because I knew what it was like to lose your only remaining family.

I was glad she wasn't Tanner's heartbreaker because I actually liked this woman.

She looked like the girl next door, and she was obviously intelligent. Tanner apparently cared about her, which was good enough for me.

"You grew up here?" I asked in a friendlier tone.

"I did," she said as she opened her lunch box. "I left about eleven years ago to go to college. I got a PhD in economics. I'm a market

180

researcher in Boston, but I really want to move back to Crystal Fork. Tanner is trying to help me find a place so I can move back permanently."

"So you're actually Doctor Collier," I mused.

Okay, this woman was beyond intelligent if she had an advanced degree in economics.

She wrinkled her nose. "No one calls me that except when I'm at work, and honestly, I don't think Tanner has realized yet that I'm a grown up. He still treats me like I'm a child, even though he's only ten years older than I am. I adore him, but he can be incredibly annoying at times."

I laughed. "I'm starting to think every Remington brother is extremely overprotective of the people they care about. I'm Anna by the way. I've been staying with Kaleb, but I'll be going back to Los Angeles soon."

"Because you have to perform at the awards show," she said in an awed tone. "I saw the commercials about your upcoming performance. You don't have to use your cover story with me. I already know that you're Annelise."

My eyes went wide as I stared at her. "Tanner told you?"

She shook her head as she chewed and swallowed a bite of her sandwich. "No," she finally said adamantly. "Tanner would never betray a secret. I saw you at The Mug And Jug a few days ago when you were there to get coffee with Kaleb. I recognized you. I'm a huge fan of your music. But I'd never tell anyone. Do you prefer to be called Anna or is that part of that whole cover story, too?"

"I do go by Anna with people I know, so I'd be happy if you'd use that name, too. How do you know about the cover story?" I asked curiously.

I really didn't mind that this woman knew the truth. I didn't know her, but I got the feeling she could keep a secret. She'd known for a few days, and apparently hadn't told anyone.

"You're joking, right?" she asked as she shot me a small smile. "This is Crystal Fork. Everyone talks about anyone new in town. I've heard all about you and Kaleb already. Honestly, I suspect that

I'm not the only one who knows your true identity, but this town protects their residents and anyone close to them."

I had to wonder if she was right. Were there other people who actually knew that I was Annelise?

"Thanks for keeping my secret," I said gratefully. "I don't have much time left here with Kaleb, and I'd rather I didn't have reporters breathing down our necks."

"You have a right to your privacy, Anna," she answered. "And I like Kaleb. He's always been so nice to me. He and Devon have always made me feel like I'm part of the Remington family, even though I'm not. You found yourself an amazing man."

It made sense that she knew all of the Remington brothers if she was close to Tanner and she'd grown up here.

"All of the Remington brothers are good guys," I pointed out.

She took a sip of the water she'd pulled out of the bag a few minutes ago before she replied, "I might argue about Devon being included if I didn't know him. But he's one of the good guys, too. He just hides it well sometimes."

I laughed. "I personally think he's full of shit. I think he has a good heart."

"He does," Lauren agreed. "So are you and Kaleb an item? Tanner hasn't given me the scoop, and I try not to really listen to the town gossip."

I smiled at her. Since she was so close to Tanner, I saw no reason to lie. "I guess you could say we are."

Because I was comfortable with her, I told her how we met and how I ended up here in Crystal Fork.

"God, I'm so sorry about your parents," she said with genuine remorse in her voice. "I heard about it in the news months ago. I should have told you that right from the beginning. It took me a long time to get my head on straight after Keith died. I can only imagine how difficult this is for you. How are you doing with their deaths now?"

She was so nice that I opened up to her. "I'm doing okay. Better than I was a few months ago. Kaleb has been there for me when I didn't have anyone else to talk to about it."

"If anyone would understand, it's Kaleb," Lauren said solemnly. "It was hard for all of them when they lost their dad."

"I know. Maybe that's why it was so easy to talk to him about it and cry on his shoulder for a while," I said thoughtfully.

"I'm really glad Kaleb was there for you when you needed him," Lauren said earnestly.

I still needed Kaleb, but not in the same way I did weeks ago.

"I guess I'll get to see you both at the goodbye party," she added. "Tanner invited me. I'm not leaving for Boston until next Tuesday."

I'd actually just found out that I was having a goodbye party. I'd spoken to Kaleb's mother about the barbecue right before I'd left the house.

"Why didn't you talk to Kaleb when you saw me at The Mug And Jug?" I questioned.

"He looked extremely preoccupied," she said with a small laugh. "He didn't even know I was there. I don't think he saw anyone except you. He's crazy about you, Anna."

"I'm pretty crazy about him, too," I confessed. "But this relationship is going to be really complicated. I have my life in California, and he has to be here."

"You'll work it out. You're in love with him, right?"

Her words hit me like a ton of bricks.

I stared at her blankly, confused for a moment.

"I'm sorry," she said remorsefully. "Was that a little too personal?"

I shook my head, flustered. "No. It's not that. Kaleb and I really haven't known each other that long."

"I'm not sure it takes a long time to fall in love with the right person," she said softly. "I think when you meet that person, you instinctively know that it feels right. It might not seem rational or wise to blurt those words out too soon, so we leave those words unsaid and unrecognized longer than necessary."

Everything Lauren had just said was probably true. Honestly, I'd probably known that I was in love with Kaleb Remington for a while now. Everything did feel right when we were together. I just hadn't wanted to admit it to myself.

"You're just figuring out that you love him," Lauren guessed.

I nodded slowly. "I think I probably already knew, but I didn't put a name to those emotions. Maybe I thought if I actually did admit it, that it would make it harder for me to leave. That might not make sense—"

"Believe me, it makes a lot of sense to me," she commiserated. "Your heart is safe with him, Anna. Kaleb would never intentionally hurt you. I've known him for a long time, and I've never seen him look at another woman the way he looks at you."

"I know he'd never intentionally hurt me," I said in a barely audible voice, still stunned from finally putting the words to my emotions and how I felt about Kaleb.

"Everything you've said to me will never be revealed to anyone," Lauren reassured me softly.

I nodded again.

For some reason, I trusted her, and I wasn't a woman who trusted easily.

However, I usually trusted my instincts, and I could sense an inherent kindness and empathy in Lauren that I didn't see all that often in my world.

I decided right then and there that Lauren Collier and I were definitely going to be friends.

# Chapter 26

*Kaleb*

Anna wasn't home when I got there, and I'd arrived later than I expected.

I'd stopped by my mother's home for a brief visit on the way to my place since I hadn't seen her for a while.

I already knew that Anna hadn't been at Mom's ranch, and that would generally be the first place I would go to look for her.

I'd searched the house, trying not to jump to conclusions, but I still remembered what had happened to Shelby when I'd lost track of her for a very brief period of time.

Anna was a high-profile celebrity, and whoever owned that shell company was probably pissed off right now because they were no longer getting funds from her.

Her parents had been murdered in cold blood and that murderer was still on the loose.

Maybe I'd like to think she was safe here, but that wasn't really the case.

In some ways, it would be easier to get to Anna here than in the middle of Los Angeles where there were people everywhere.

Impatiently, I ripped off my suit jacket and tie, tossing them onto the kitchen table before I left the house and headed out to the barn.

I wasn't sure if I was relieved or more worried when I saw that Bella wasn't in her stall.

If she wasn't at Mom's ranch, where in the hell did she go?

Maybe she had ridden into Crystal Fork, but she usually texted me if she was going there to see if there was anything I wanted or needed in town.

I was about to tack up my gelding to go look for her when I felt my phone vibrate in the pocket of my pants.

I reached for it, and all of the tension suddenly left my body as I read the message.

**Anna:** *If you're home, I'm on my way. I'll be there in a few minutes. I wanted to have lunch at the river because it's such a beautiful day.*

I gripped the phone with more force than was necessary.

"She's fine, idiot," I grumbled to myself as I walked to the open barn door. "She was taking in the fucking outdoors."

My gut continued to roll, but I tried to calm my ass down as I saw Bella and Anna approaching from the direction of the river.

Rationally, it made sense that she'd go out for a ride in nice weather like this, but I wasn't all that reasonable right now.

*Christ!* I'd jumped to the worst-case scenario, seeing visions of her being kidnapped or murdered in broad daylight.

I didn't say a word to Anna as I helped her down from Bella's back and automatically started to take off the horse's tack.

I couldn't say anything to her right now.

If I said something, it was going to be words that I'd probably want to take back later.

Anna shot me a puzzled look as she removed Bella's bridle and put it away while I tended to the saddle.

"Kaleb?" she said in a hesitant voice as she watched me rub down her horse.

"Don't, Anna," I said roughly. "Not right now. You scared the shit out of me when I got home and you were gone without letting me know where you went. Give me a little space right now."

I was being a total dick.

I knew it, but I couldn't stop myself right now.

Anna wasn't a normal female, and it was possible that she was a target of a murderer.

"I'm sorry," she murmured as she turned around and headed toward the house without another word.

I'd asked her to give me some space, and she'd done exactly what I wanted.

I couldn't talk about her disappearing act right now, especially not in this barn where I had so many bad memories of coming here and finding Shelby gone without a trace.

I took my time getting Bella back in her stall and tending to the horse's needs before I headed for the house.

My mind was still racing with all of the things that could have happened to Anna when I entered through the kitchen door and saw her putting away the clean dishes in the dishwasher.

She turned her head to look at me. "Feeling better?" she asked cautiously.

Hell, she was probably afraid of what I was going to say, and I hated that guarded look on her face.

"No," I answered bluntly as I approached her.

She closed the dishwasher and faced me without a single bit of fear in her eyes.

If I had to name the look in her eyes, I'd say it was deep concern.

"I should have texted you where I was going," she said calmly. "If I wasn't going to text you earlier, then I should have been back before you got home. That was my plan, but I ran into Lauren at the river and we started talking. Time got away from me. I'm used to being alone and not having anyone who worries about me. When you went to the barn, you probably had flashbacks of what happened when Shelby was kidnapped."

I crowded her against the counter. "Yes and no," I said in an agitated tone.

Yes, I *had* thought about what had happened to Shelby, but this time, my concern was *all* about Anna.

She entwined her arms around my neck. "I'm fine, Kaleb. Nothing happened."

She put a hand on the back of my head and pulled me down to kiss me. It was like she knew exactly what I needed, and I kissed her like the desperate man I was right now.

When we finally came up for air, she calmly slipped out of the shorts she was wearing and her panties, and then undid my suit pants until she had her hand wrapped around my extremely hard cock.

Even though I was agitated, there would probably never be a time that I wouldn't get hard when I saw Anna stripping off her clothes.

She pulled me down to kiss me again without another word, hopped up to wrap her legs around my hips, and ground against me.

At that moment, I completely snapped.

I surged inside her slick, tight heat, my heart thumping against my chest wall with all the adrenaline that had built up inside my body. I gripped her beautiful ass, moved to the wall of the kitchen, and fucked her like a madman who had just lost any sense of sanity.

It was rough and completely devoid of anything blatantly sexual.

The carnal act was more about reaffirming that Anna was mine and that she was safe, healthy, and here…with me.

I gripped her ass so hard that she'd probably have bruises the next day, but I was focused on one goal.

*Mine!*

Anna Kendrick was fucking mine!

And I wanted to reassure myself that she'd always be mine and safe with me.

"Yes!" Anna moaned as her fingernails dug into my dress shirt, clutching me like she needed the same damn thing.

She wasn't afraid of this brutal claiming of her body.

She embraced it thoroughly, encouraged it, which made me even more insane.

I braced her back against the wall and pounded into her like a guy who had completely lost his mind.

Every thrust into her welcoming pussy made me feel so fucking alive again that I was determined to watch, hear, and feel her come apart in my arms just to assure myself that she felt the same damn way.

"Touch yourself, Anna," I demanded between my rampant strokes inside her. "I need to feel you coming around my cock right now."

I wasn't going to last much longer, and I couldn't stop. I needed her to send herself over the edge this time.

"Yes!" she hissed and immediately shoved her hand between our bodies, and started to stroke her slick clit roughly.

I knew she was as lost as I was in this madness, and I fucking loved the way she went after exactly what she wanted.

She wanted *me*.

She wanted *this*.

And she fiercely wanted that orgasm she was reaching for right now.

I leaned into her and nipped the soft flesh at the bottom of her neck harder than I'd meant to, and then soothed the small mark with my tongue.

I felt it the moment before she reached her breaking point.

I was starting to know Anna's body as well as I knew my own.

She leaned her head back and screamed. "Oh, my God. Kaleb!"

*Fuck!* There was nothing like hearing her scream my name when she'd reached her climax.

I was addicted to hearing and seeing her find her release while she shuddered in my arms.

She didn't hold back anything from me anymore, and I felt so goddamn lucky that she trusted me that much.

Her powerful orgasm milked my cock beautifully, and I lost the last of my control and shot off inside her as I buried myself deep, exactly where I needed to be right now.

"Anna," I groaned, her name almost ripped from my throat as I had one of the most powerful and longest orgasms I'd ever experienced.

*Mine!*

Hell, maybe I'd always known that Anna was the one woman who could make me completely lose my head, but I just hadn't admitted how much I needed her.

B. A. Scott

She'd completely filled the void I'd been feeling at the cabin, the restlessness that I'd never been able to put a finger on until I'd met her.

*She'd* been everything that had been missing from my life.

As crazy as it might sound, Anna made all of my life make sense to me.

Yeah, it was complicated, but I no longer gave a shit if she complicated my life to the point of madness.

As long as she was with me in all of that craziness.

I moved to the counter and gently sat her naked ass down on top of it, wrapping my arms protectively around her body as she recovered from her climax.

She lowered her forehead onto my shoulder. She continued to take deep breaths as both of our heart rates slowed back down to normal.

I'd been extremely rough with her, and I knew I should be apologizing, but I didn't.

Something told me that she'd needed that as much as I had.

Hell, she'd actually initiated it in the first place, but I wondered if she'd known that she was unleashing a beast when she'd palmed my cock like that.

"Too rough?" I finally questioned hoarsely as I threaded my fingers into her silky hair and stroked her scalp.

I felt her shake her head adamantly against my shoulder.

Anna was rarely wordless, but if she was as affected by what had just happened as I was, maybe she wasn't ready to speak.

"No," she finally whispered wholeheartedly.

"Good," I said, finally satisfied that she was okay. "Next time, it might be better if you text me or leave a note and let me know where you're going."

## Chapter 27

*Anna*

"Lauren said something to me at the river today," I informed Kaleb as we drove back from town. "It has me wondering if it might be true."

We'd gone to grab a burger for dinner since neither one of us felt like cooking after that crazy encounter in the kitchen.

"What did she say?" he asked as he expertly navigated the back roads to get to his house.

"She knew who I was almost immediately because she's a fan of my music. She saw us one day in town at The Mug And Jug. She mentioned that maybe some of the other people in town know who I am, too, but they were keeping my secret. Do you think that's true?"

"I'm almost sure that's probably true," Kaleb mused.

"You do?" I said in a surprised voice. "Why didn't you tell me?"

"Because I don't know that for a fact," he replied. "But I know the people in this town. I was never worried about the majority of them recognizing you. I was more concerned that someone who didn't care much about the people in Crystal Fork might. It's a pretty tight community, but it's gotten bigger over the years. A lot of the residents will gossip amongst themselves, but they'd still protect the subject of that gossip from anyone outside the community."

"Do you think they feel like I'm one of them?"

I'd fallen in love with Crystal Fork and many of the people here, so I waited curiously for his answer.

"Absolutely," he said like he didn't have a doubt in his mind. "You were with me in the beginning, so that automatically made you someone worth protecting. Now, I think they feel like you're one of their own because you're so damn nice to all of them."

I smiled. "They're nice to me. I love it here."

Crystal Fork had started to feel like home to me, and I hadn't been this relaxed or comfortable in a long time.

I'd managed to write more songs than I could possibly produce in California, even though I'd been slacking off with Kaleb.

"Living in a small town has its problems, too," Kaleb informed me. "Everyone usually knows your business, especially if you don't make any effort to conceal your business. The amount of gossip flying around is ridiculous, and sometimes it's not based on real facts."

"But there's so much good in this town that it can make you overlook the bad things," I told him. "People treat you like extended family, and they go out of their way to be helpful."

"That's why I still live here," Kaleb told me.

I leaned my head back against the headrest and released a long breath. "It's hard to believe that there's a place where people still try to protect their neighbors. It's not like that in the city."

"Is that what you meant earlier when you said that you were used to being alone and not having anyone who watched out for you?" he questioned.

"Yes," I told him wistfully. "I've lived in my home in Beverly Hills for eight years now, and I don't even know my neighbors. People keep to themselves there. If I did go missing, nobody would really care or notice except for Kim. As long as I showed up for performances and met my obligations, nobody really cared what I did unless I was paying them to make my safety their business."

"Except for Ray," he reminded me in an irritated tone.

"I think Ray only cares because I'm a cash cow for him. He's worried about his own financial security. Maybe that's harsh, but I think it's true. He's not worried about my safety or my well-being."

"I'm glad you finally noticed that," Kaleb said in a gentler tone.

"Maybe I wanted to think that he cared about me as a friend because he cared about my dad, but he's changed a lot over the years."

"I care, Anna," he said gruffly. "I do give a shit about your happiness and your well-being."

"I know that," I said softly. "I shouldn't have left without leaving a note or letting you know where I was, but I've been alone for a long time."

"Fuck!" Kaleb rasped. "I don't want to strangle you to death with my fears, but we don't know who murdered your parents, and you are a high-profile pop star. You'll always be vulnerable to some crazy ass and delusional people in the world."

"I guess I feel safe here," I told him honestly.

"Normally, you would be safe here," Kaleb grumbled. "I just don't like not knowing where you are in case you need help. Being famous puts you at risk, Anna."

"I'd feel the same way if our positions were reversed," I admitted.

In some ways, it wasn't just Crystal Fork that made me feel safe here.

It was Kaleb.

It was strange knowing that somebody actually cared about me and my safety now, not because I was a famous pop star, but because he cared about *me*.

I loved this man so much that it was almost painful, but it was way too early to blurt that out to him.

This whole relationship was so new that I didn't want to tell him that I loved him and have him look at me like I was crazy for feeling that way so soon.

He cared about me.

I cared about him.

That was enough...for now.

"I'll text you and let you know where I am next time," I promised.

"If you don't, you'll end up manhandled by a crazy man again," he said drily.

"In that case, I might be tempted to sneak away every single day. I like being *manhandled* by you."

I'd sensed exactly what Kaleb had needed earlier, and I loved every moment of it.

We'd always had hot, mind-blowing sex, but that particular encounter had nothing to do with sex and everything to do with the way we were connected.

Yeah, it had been carnal and rough, but I'd desperately needed that reassurance, too.

I had been feeling a little vulnerable because I'd just recognized that I was madly in love with Kaleb.

I'd wanted to feel every emotion he was feeling at that moment because I'd been feeling the same way.

Raw.

Defenseless.

Scared.

And exposed.

"Don't test me, Anna," he said gruffly. "I'd probably put you over my knee and slap your ass until you begged for forgiveness."

He was joking, but…

"I might like that, too," I said playfully.

"Fuck! I'm driving right now, Anna," he said in a warning voice.

A shiver of awareness ran down my spine.

I actually giggled. "And you're doing a very fine job of that. You haven't hit a deer yet."

It was almost dark, and the deer were everywhere, but I'd discovered that Kaleb was an expert at spotting them before they ended up right in front of his truck.

"Smartass," he rumbled.

"That's one of the things you like the most about me," I informed him. "I'm not scared off by your power or your wealth."

"Unfortunately, that's probably true," he admitted grudgingly.

"Then I can admit that your alpha male bossiness turns me on sometimes," I said in a sultry voice that I knew made him crazy. "Not to mention that hot body and your very large, hard—"

"Anna!" he said dangerously. "You'll pay for this later."

"I know," I said boldly. "I'm looking forward to it."

He let the curse words fly as he turned into the driveway.

I smiled, but I knew I wasn't going to be laughing about this later.

He'd make me pay in the most erotic ways possible, and I'd love every moment of it.

He stopped in the driveway instead of pulling into the garage.

We got out of the truck and Kaleb took my hand. "I want to show you something before we go in."

I followed him curiously as we walked toward the barn.

He took me into a space I'd never seen before or explored.

"My woodworking shop that I never used," he explained as he flipped the lights on.

He led me across the room and stopped in front of a beautiful, handmade table.

There were things about it that reminded me of the table he'd made at the cabin, but it was also completely unique.

"You need a coffee table in your music room, next to your piano. I know you won't put your coffee on the piano. I thought this might work."

I was touched because he actually remembered me saying that I wouldn't put my coffee on that beautiful grand piano. I was afraid I'd knock it over and end up with coffee streaming everywhere over and into that gorgeous instrument.

I ran my free hand over the smooth surface of the beautiful creation.

It was round, just high enough to work next to the piano, and it had my name carved into the wood, along with some carefully constructed musical notes.

He'd stained it light gray with purple accents that were distressed and blended into the design very subtly and perfectly.

Purple was my favorite color, and he'd obviously remembered me mentioning that, too.

The craftsmanship of the table was amazing, and I thought it was the most beautiful piece of furniture I'd ever seen.

It would look amazing in the music room.

"I wanted you to see it before you go because it's a gift to you," he said huskily. "I still have to do some work on it, so it won't be done before you leave."

Tears spilled from my eyes and down my cheeks.

Kaleb wrapped his arm around my waist. "Hey, this isn't supposed to make you cry. I thought you'd like it because you refuse to set your coffee on the grand piano."

I wrapped my arms around his neck and hopped up, knowing that Kaleb would grab my ass to keep me steady. "It's absolutely beautiful," I said with a happy sob. "I think it's the best gift I've ever received. I thought you stopped woodworking."

He'd obviously found time to work on the table while I was writing music or when he made those long trips out to the barn in the evening.

It was so thoughtful and sweet that I couldn't help bawling all over him.

He probably didn't realize that people didn't usually give me gifts this personal.

I snuggled into his warmth, getting as close as possible to this thoughtful man.

He chuckled. "I thought Mom's picture was your best gift ever."

"It's still in the top two," I shared. "But this is definitely the best."

"I actually haven't done any woodworking in years," Kaleb said contemplatively. "I guess your creativity inspired me. Or maybe it was just you who inspired me. I'm glad you like it."

I lifted my hand and swiped the tears from my face. "Thank you. I know how valuable your free time is, Kaleb. You'll probably never know how much this means to me."

I leaned down and kissed him, pouring all the love and affection I had for him into that kiss.

When I finally lifted my head, he grinned at me. "If that's my reward, I'm making furniture for you for the entire house."

I loved the way that he just assumed that his home was my home, too.

He'd made that table for the music room, a room that he always referred to as *my* music room. Just like he referred to that beautiful grand piano as *my* piano.

I moved my hips against his very hard erection. "I think you'll be a little too busy to be making more furniture. But I love the table."

He slapped my ass playfully. "Behave," he warned me.

"Never," I said with a happy laugh as I buried my face in the side of his neck and nipped his skin.

He grinned. "Fuck! You make me happy, Anna, even if you are a very bad girl."

My heart squeezed inside my chest. Kaleb made me happy, too. So much so that I couldn't really express it in words. "I'd think I'd really like to see how you handle bad girls right now."

"Done!" he answered in a husky voice and proceeded to carry me all the way back to the house.

## Chapter 28

*Kaleb*

I really hated attending a goodbye party when I was trying like hell to stay in denial about Anna leaving the next day.

Nevertheless, I was here, and so was Anna.

I watched her as she fluttered around my mother's backyard, talking to every person present like she was honored that they'd shown up just for her.

Hell, she probably did feel lucky that everyone who had been invited had come to the barbecue.

Unfortunately, I felt like I was in hell.

"I know it's a goodbye party, but you look like you're at a funeral, boy," Silas said as he walked up to my location near the house. "You're pretty sad that she's leaving, huh?"

I took a slug of the beer I was holding and then I looked at the older man suspiciously.

I liked Silas. I'd known him since I was a kid. That was probably why I already knew that he had something on his mind.

I really hoped it wasn't more advice.

I was in a foul mood at the moment, which was why I was standing here alone.

"Are you worried that she might forget you when she's back in California with all those other superstars?" he asked curiously.

My gaze shot toward him, and I lifted a brow.

"I might be old," he said crankily. "But I'm not stupid. I'll admit that it took me a while to place where I'd seen that face before, but I put it all together within a couple of days. She's Annelise."

I nodded. If he'd known about Anna's real identity for that long, I wasn't going to deny it.

Eventually, I hoped that Anna would be back in Crystal Fork often, and the people in this town were going to know exactly who she was, if they didn't already.

"I assumed that some people would figure it out," I told him.

"Most of them have nothing better to do than gossip. There's not a lot going on in this town," Silas pointed out. "There's a few that know the truth. The smart ones like me. I like her. Always have. I kind of hoped she'd decide to stay."

"That's not possible, Silas," I said flatly. "Anna has her own life in California, and her music is important to her."

"Anything is possible," he contradicted as he ran a hand over his silver beard. "I don't think Anna really belongs in her old life anymore. I don't think she was happy there."

"She lost both of her parents," I told him. "She was grieving."

"I heard about that," he informed me. "But I think her unhappiness was more than just grief. After her parents died, there was probably no one around who cared about her anymore. It must have been lonely for her."

"She has millions of adoring fans," I explained.

"Annelise has millions of adoring fans," he corrected. "Anna must have been lonely. I hate that."

Hell, what could I say? I hated it, too.

"Your mama is pretty fond of her, just like the rest of us," Silas mentioned.

"I know," I acknowledged a little irritably. "What do you want me to do? Kidnap her and make her stay?"

My mother had made her displeasure known about Anna leaving. Yeah, she understood that Anna had to go, but she was definitely not happy about it.

Silas's eyes lit up. "Now that's a thought."

"No," I said firmly. "Anna and I will still see each other, and I'd rather she didn't hate me for kidnapping her."

"Do you want my advice?" he asked.

It was a rhetorical question. Whether I wanted his advice or not, he was going to give it to me.

"I really wish you wouldn't," I said, even though I knew those words were useless.

"If you love her, I think you should marry that girl," Silas said like he'd never heard my protest.

*If I love her?*

Hell, I'd probably gone head over heels for Anna in the very beginning, but I'd just recently admitted to myself that I loved her. Right after I'd lost my shit in the kitchen because I'd been terrified that something bad had happened to her.

I was fairly certain that I was destined to meet Anna and fall in love with her, and I didn't fucking believe in fate.

*At all.*

"That would be interesting," I commented to Silas. "She lives in California, and I live in Montana."

I wasn't about to tell Silas that I was in love with Anna.

He could keep a secret, but he'd hound me about marrying her forever.

I didn't really want to share the way I felt about Anna with anyone yet.

"That's just geography, boy," Silas said, disgusted. "Love isn't always perfect."

I was relieved when Anna strode up to us, looking gorgeous in a pretty sundress she'd bought in town.

I was almost jealous when she gave Silas a very genuine, enthusiastic hug.

"I was looking for you, Silas," she told the older man. "I wanted to thank you for all those coffees you made me, and the occasional advice."

*Occasional?*

Silas gave advice every minute of the day.

But it was obvious that Anna adored Silas, and the feelings were mutual.

Honestly, when Silas wasn't giving unwanted advice, he was a hard man not to like.

He gave a shit about the town of Crystal Fork and most of the people in it.

I wasn't surprised that Silas had gotten so attached to Anna.

Everyone in this town loved Anna.

Including…me.

Silas beamed at Anna. "When are you coming back to see me?"

Anna shot me a questioning look. "As soon as I'm invited back," she said teasingly.

"I'm inviting you back now," Silas said adamantly. "You're more than welcome to stay with me anytime."

"If Anna comes back, she'll be staying with me," I informed Silas. "And she knows that my place is already her second home."

Okay, so maybe I'd never *directly* told her that I wanted her to come back to Montana *as often as possible*, but I'd make sure she knew that by the time she left.

Really, she should already know that. I had told her that she could come to Montana whenever she could break free, but I wasn't leaving anything to chance.

"Can I consider that my official invitation?" Anna joked.

"Yes," I replied cantankerously.

Someone called Silas's name, and he wandered off.

Anna came to me and wrapped her arms around my neck. "I feel the same way you do," she said softly. "This isn't easy for me, either."

"Fuck! I'm sorry," I said with genuine remorse.

I should be supporting her, but I was feeling sorry for myself.

"I'll miss you horribly," she said with a long sigh. "But at least I'll see you on Friday."

"I'll miss you, too," I said hoarsely. "You do realize that I want you to come back. As often as possible. Just say the word and my jet will be there to pick you up. I don't want you taking charters. Some of them don't maintenance their planes that well."

She smiled up at me. "Should I put your pilot on speed dial?"

"Yes," I said seriously.

I put my beer down on a side table and wrapped my arms around her waist.

I didn't give a damn who was watching us.

Everyone was going to know exactly how I felt about Anna at some point.

"Will you stay with me when you come for the awards show?" she asked.

I'd definitely planned on it. I wanted as much time with her as possible, and I wanted to see her home in California.

I chuckled. "I don't know. Is that an official invitation?"

She slapped my shoulder playfully. "Yes. You're always as welcome in my home as I am in yours."

I lowered my head and kissed her.

It was impossible for me to be this close to Anna and not kiss her.

I heard a cough behind Anna, and then my mother said, "I really hate to interrupt."

No, she didn't.

She actually loved to interrupt.

I ended the kiss without it being abrupt.

I wasn't a teenaged boy anymore who'd just got caught making out with the girl next door.

"Neither one of you have eaten a thing," my mother said as she shoved two plates toward us. "I made you both a plate."

Anna quickly disentangled us and reached for the plate. "Thank you, Millie. I'm starving."

The plates were loaded high with ribs, a burger, potato salad, and mac and cheese.

I took the other plate, a little annoyed that I'd had to let Anna go to do it.

"Do you have everything packed?" my mother asked Anna.

Anna nodded. "I really didn't bring much, so there wasn't much to pack. I was only supposed to be in Montana for a few days. If I could fit Bella in my suitcase, I probably would. I'll miss her."

"Then I guess you'll have to come home often to ride her," my mother replied. "I'm going to miss you terribly, Anna."

Anna put her arm around my mother. "I'll miss you, too. I promise that I'll be here as much as possible. Thank you for everything you've done for me."

A tear leaked from Mom's eye, and it made my gut ache.

It killed me to see my mother cry.

I cringed when Anna followed suit and a tear plopped onto her cheek, too.

Hell, now I was doubly screwed.

"I didn't do much," Mom said as she swiped the tear away. "You've kept *me* company."

Anna *had* seen my mother a lot. She'd made it a point to take a break during the day to go see Mom when I was working.

Their sadness was genuine.

The two women had formed a special bond in the time Anna had been here.

While my mother couldn't replace Anna's mother, she'd told me that her relationship with my mom had helped her.

I was certain that Anna had been good for my mother, too. She'd been pretty lonely since my dad had passed away, even though my brothers and I tried to see her as often as possible.

"Why is everyone crying like somebody died over here?" Devon asked as he strolled up with his own plate of food with Tanner right behind him.

"Everybody okay?" Tanner asked as he shot me a questioning look.

"We're fine," Mom replied. "We're just a little sad that Anna has to go back to California in the morning."

"She'll be back," Devon said in a comforting voice to my mother.

"You can throw a 'welcome home' party the next time she comes," Tanner suggested.

I grinned at Tanner as our mother perked up again.

He knew exactly what to say to make our mother feel better.

Mom loved to throw parties, picnics, and barbecues.

She smiled at Tanner. "I'll start planning that party as soon as she leaves."

With Tanner and Devon present, the conversation became a little more upbeat, and they had Anna and Mom laughing in a matter of minutes.

I looked at my siblings, knowing that they had come over because they'd seen that I was uncomfortable with the tears because I wasn't feeling all that upbeat myself.

The three of us might not always agree, but at the moment, I was grateful that I had two brothers who would always have my back.

## Chapter 29

*Anna*

"You don't look like a woman who's happy to be back in Southern California. You're up for multiple awards at the awards ceremony, and you don't look excited about that, either," Kim said sympathetically as I sat in her salon chair three days later.

Honestly...I wasn't.

I'd gone through the motions for my rehearsals.

I'd cleared up some other business because it was what needed to be done.

I'd been a little excited about the designer dress I was wearing for the awards show because Kaleb would see me dressed up for the first time.

But I just couldn't find much enthusiasm for anything else right now.

"You're missing your man," Kim stated.

I met her eyes in the mirror and nodded. "I don't know what's wrong with me," I shared. "I just feel...different."

"Probably because you got a taste of what it's like to live a semi normal life with someone you love," she commented as she tilted my head back and put wax on my eyebrows. "You've spent your entire life dancing to other people's tunes. What did it feel like to be away from all that?"

The shop was empty, so Kim and I were able to talk freely.

She always took me in after hours.

I didn't even flinch as she ripped the tape off my eyebrow.

I was used to it.

I'd spent a lot of my time sitting in this very chair, trying to look perfect for some performance.

"It felt good. Really good," I confessed. "Other than you, I missed absolutely nothing about my life here."

"That's because this life doesn't fit you anymore, Anna. I don't think it ever really did," she observed as she carefully waxed my other eyebrow. "You've just gone with the flow, but can you really say you've ever been happy? You've been all over the world, but you haven't really seen those countries because you're on to the next show. Sometimes you hibernate for weeks at your house because you have to write music. There's no joy in your life, baby girl. I've been worried about you for a long time. I wasn't really surprised when you had that meltdown. I think your parents were the only ones who really cared about you, other than me. All of the other people who surround you sometimes are bloodsuckers. They suck the life out of you."

"I miss my mom and dad," I said wistfully. "I think I always will. I went to their gravesites as soon as I got to Montana. It was really hard for me to leave, just like it was hard for me to leave them after the burial."

My parents had been buried outside of Bozeman in our hometown because that was what they'd wanted.

I'd felt compelled to get back to that cemetery as soon as I'd stepped into Montana.

"It was hard because you didn't really have a place to go grieve," Kim said gently.

What if he wasn't in love with me and the entire relationship just fizzled out over time?

Yeah, I already knew that wasn't going to happen on my end. I was in love with Kaleb. But I had no idea how he'd feel next month or next year.

"Now tell me what we're doing with this hair," Kim said as she finished my eyebrows and started to fluff my hair. "Back to Annelise?"

It was odd how I now thought of Anna and Annelise as two separate people, especially after spending time being myself in Montana.

Annelise was nothing more than a made-up person that I'd learned to portray well over the years.

She was a brand I'd worked hard to cultivate, but other than the music, we had very little in common. I hadn't really thought about that until I'd spent time in Montana just being me.

While there were some artists who could be their authentic self and still be famous, that wasn't what had happened to me.

Somehow, I'd lost some of myself to be Annelise.

My Annelise image *wasn't* all Anna.

Maybe it was beyond time for me to blend the two together into one person.

"I think I'd really prefer to just keep being me," I told Kim as I looked into the mirror. "I like my natural color and the shorter style. If people stop listening to my music because of the way I look or who I am as a person, I guess they really weren't ever a fan of my music."

"Good choice," she said approvingly. "You actually look even more gorgeous this way, and the cut is in trend. Should we do some subtle highlights just to make the color pop? It would look fantastic with your eyes and that gorgeous dress you're wearing Saturday."

I smiled at her. "I don't want to be the old Annelise, but that doesn't mean I don't want to look good for the awards show."

"No one will be able to take their eyes off you," Kim said as she smiled back at me mischievously. "I am your stylist extraordinaire."

"I'll have some stunning jewelry to wear Saturday," I told Kim. "Kaleb sent a platinum and diamond necklace and earrings yesterday by special delivery. They're beautiful and so unique. I like them better than the jewelry that was offered on loan from the jewelers to go with the dress. I don't think he meant for me to wear them to this particular event, but I'm wearing them."

Kim lifted an eyebrow. "What? No photos?"

She stopped messing with my hair for a moment while I reached for my phone.

"I took one to send to Kaleb so he could make sure I got the right items," I said as I brought up the photo.

Kim grabbed my phone, and her eyes widened as she looked at the jewelry. "Oh, dear God," she exclaimed. "It's beautiful, but I don't think I want to even guess how much they cost. There has to be a gazillion carats of diamonds in that jewelry. Your man has incredible taste. And they're definitely your style."

"I know," I answered as I took the phone back and put it away. "I could hardly refuse a personal gift like that, but he must have spent a fortune on that jewelry."

I wore a lot of expensive jewelry for big events, but that jewelry was just a loan from designers who wanted the cache or promotion of me wearing their designs.

I'd never spent that kind of money on jewelry I owned, and I'd never received a gift like that.

"He's a billionaire, Anna," Kim reminded me as she went back to work on my hair. "And you're a high-profile woman who does a lot of events. He has the money. Let him spoil you rotten. You deserve it."

"That's the problem," I said with a sigh. "He's a billionaire. I'd like to give him something special, too, but he has everything. I decided to put together a video slideshow of the pictures I took in Montana for him. I did a lot of selfies with him, and took a bunch of photos of everyone at the barbecue. I wrote the music to put with the video. It's not a very exciting gift considering how much he's given me, but there's nothing material I can give him that he doesn't already have."

"I think that's a really thoughtful idea," Kim replied. "I don't think people with a lot of money care about getting material things. You spent your time and creativeness on that project, just like he spent time and energy making you a table that cost him almost nothing, but it meant everything to you. I'm sure he's going to love it."

"I hope so," I told her. "I should be able to finish it up tomorrow. I'll email it to him as soon as I'm done."

"For two people who are so far apart, you think about each other a lot," Kim observed.

I nodded as she continued to put highlights in my hair.

Kaleb Remington had become a huge part of my life.

It was absolutely impossible *not* to think about him when he was so damn far away.

## Chapter 30

*Kaleb*

I'd played the video that Anna had sent me more times than I wanted to admit.

All I could think about when I'd played it over and over again was how much she must have put into it...for me.

I'd recognized the fact that the music was Anna's almost immediately. I recognized her style and the way she played the piano now.

That damn video was the only thing that had gotten me through that last day before I finally saw Anna's beautiful face again in person.

She'd picked me up at the airport Friday evening, and we'd spent the night making up for lost time before we'd gone to the awards show the next day.

The event had been pretentious except for the parts where Anna had won her well-deserved awards and had performed magically.

"Do you always get sick like that before you perform?" I asked her as we were headed back to her home in a limousine.

I'd been with her in her dressing room before her performance, where she'd changed from the gorgeous dress she'd been wearing into a stage costume.

I'd been alarmed when she'd promptly vomited her guts out before going on stage, and it had scared the hell out of me.

She'd treated the whole episode like it was normal and had blown it off as nerves. She'd simply brushed her teeth, fixed anything that was disheveled, and gone out on stage.

"Always," she confessed. "I told you that I have terrible stage fright. I always get sick right before a performance."

*Fuck!* No wonder she hated performing live in front of large crowds.

If I had to get violently sick like that all the time, I would have quit a long time ago.

"You were amazing. Have I told you how beautiful you look tonight?"

She was breathtaking.

Anna had decided not to change her hair back to the old Annelise style, and I was secretly happy that she hadn't.

She still looked like Anna, but she'd performed like Annelise.

While I loved the formfitting red dress she was wearing, I'd wanted to punch every guy who had looked at her like they were fantasizing about fucking her.

There had been many of those men throughout the night.

*Christ!* I knew that was something I was going to have to get used to because I was with Annelise, but it made me totally insane.

My only consolation was that Anna didn't seem to notice that other men were staring at her like they wanted to get her naked.

She was apparently so used to it that it didn't even affect her anymore.

Her gaze had always met mine with a look of adoration that had calmed my ass down a little.

The dress was sleeveless, low-cut almost to her navel, and obviously tailormade for her body. It had a small train that had made her look like a sexy princess.

I loved the fact that she'd chosen to wear the jewelry I'd given her instead of a loaned set from a jewelry designer.

I'd spent the entire night as hard as a rock. Luckily, the pants of my tuxedo were roomy enough to hide that affliction.

Anna finally answered, "Probably as many times as I've told you how handsome you look in a tuxedo. Thank you for being my date tonight."

"I wouldn't have missed it."

I meant that, even though it wasn't my scene. This event had been important to her and her career. Therefore, it was important to me, and I'd wanted to be there to support her success and to see her perform.

Although, I probably could have skipped her being sick.

It killed me to see Anna *that* nervous and physically ill, even though she'd brushed it off like it was nothing.

"Your agent wasn't there tonight," I observed.

I'd met a lot of people who were associated with Anna's career, but not Ray.

She shrugged her bare shoulders. "He wasn't invited, and I haven't seen him in person because you asked me not to right now. Ray is still hounding me about not signing over my finances to someone else. A lot. He wants to keep doing it. Maybe he needs the money I pay him for doing it, but he's called me to the point of harassment. He's always been pushy, but he's hostile right now."

"So, you haven't met up with him at all?" I asked.

I had asked Anna not to see him in person, and she'd agreed that it was something she had no desire to do in the near future.

"No," she replied. "I actually haven't seen him in person for a long time. Not since my parents' funeral. We usually just communicate by phone. I was actually surprised that he'd hounded me so much about my location when I was in Montana."

"I think it's time for you to find a new agent," I said gruffly.

"I think you're right, but it's hard to let go of someone who meant so much to my parents."

"Have you officially transferred that money?"

She nodded. "Yesterday. It was really hard to make a decision on who to use. You suggested some very good possibilities, but it's all settled now."

"Do you feel like you have more control of your money now?" I asked.

"Thanks to you," she answered. "At least I know enough to understand when they're using all those financial terms."

Anna was an intelligent woman. She picked up on a lot of the basics of investing, even though she'd claimed to be mathematically challenged.

The abrupt sound of Anna's cell phone ringing halted our conversation.

She pulled out her phone from her purse, and looked at the number.

"It's the police," she said in a puzzled voice.

I understood why she was a little confused.

It was really late. We'd attended an after party for a short time after the awards ceremony because it was being thrown by her record label.

She picked up the call immediately.

I couldn't see her face well in the dim light of the limo, but I was pretty sure I knew exactly what was happening from the tone of her stressed out answers as the conversation went on for a long time before she finally ended the call.

I'd only caught her end of the conversation, and she hadn't spoken nearly as much as the person on the other end of the call.

I pulled her closer to me and wrapped an arm around her waist. "What happened?"

Her voice was tremulous as she answered, "They caught my parents' murderer. Oh, God, Kaleb. It was Ray. It was *all* Ray. The shell company. The missing money, and their murders. His DNA was everywhere in the house and on my parents' bodies, but he'd told the police he'd been at their house the morning of the murders. He said he hugged them both before he left. That DNA was explained away at first because he was close to my parents. He was in a lot of financial trouble, and the detective told me that he had also developed a heavy cocaine habit. He was desperate for even more funds. The detective suspects that he was looking for me so he could murder me, too, before I caught on to the whole shell company scheme. He also thinks that's why they were killed. My dad probably did catch on to the swindle, and confronted Ray about it the day my parents were killed."

She stopped speaking as a cry of emotional pain left her throat.

I pulled her onto my lap and held her as she sobbed against my shoulder.

She was in shock, and I fucking hated this for her, even though I'd seen it coming.

It all made sense to me. Someone had suggested that investment, and the only person her parents would have trusted was Ray.

I'd contacted the detective on the case about my suspicions the moment after Anna had boarded my plane for California. She'd told me about those phone calls from Ray about him wanting to keep control of her finances the night before she left. At that point, everything had clicked into place for me. He'd obviously wanted to find another way to get more money out of her accounts. There was no other reason he'd want to keep handling her finances that badly. The police hadn't sounded the least bit surprised when I'd told them that I suspected Ray.

They'd obviously been investigating him for a while.

I'd asked Anna not to meet with him in person, and I'd had my security tailing him as well from the moment Anna had stepped foot in California. I'd wanted to make sure he didn't get anywhere near Anna before he was arrested.

Thank fuck she hadn't given in and told him where she was staying.

It had taken me a while to put things together. I hadn't become incredibly suspicious of him until I'd heard about those phone calls and him wanting to keep control of her finances.

Maybe I should have put things together earlier, but like Anna, I'd been blinded by the fact that Ray had meant a lot to Anna's father. Even though the guy was a pain in the ass, I'd assumed that Ray cared about her parents, too.

I hadn't known exactly when he'd finally be arrested, but I'd known the police and the feds were probably getting close.

It had torn my guts out not to be with Anna in person in case he was arrested, but I hadn't wanted to alarm her or upset her if it turned out that Ray wasn't really the guilty party.

My instincts had told me that he was guilty, and it all made sense, but I'd had no solid proof.

Apparently, the police and the feds had done their jobs and come up with the proof they needed.

"Fuck! I'm sorry, Anna," I said hoarsely as I stroked her hair.

"Did you know?" she said tearfully as her tears subsided. "Is that why you told me to stay away from meeting Ray in person?"

"I had my suspicions after you told me that he wanted to keep control of your finances," I admitted. "But I didn't want to say anything until the police and the feds knew for sure. My security team has been tracking him to make sure that he didn't come near you just in case I was right. Did they arrest the bastard?"

"H-he's d-dead," she stammered. "They tried to arrest him at his house. He shot himself before the police could make entry. Even if you'd shared your suspicions with me, I'm not sure my brain could have wrapped around that possibility. He was like an adopted son to my parents for as long as I can remember."

Which was exactly why I hadn't mentioned it to her.

Number one...I hadn't wanted to stress her out if nothing was certain.

And number two...she needed to hear that he'd been arrested before she could process that possibility.

She'd known Ray since childhood, and even if they weren't that close, she'd seen him as an annoying friend who she had known most of her life.

And she'd always accepted and respected the relationship Ray had with her parents.

"I probably should have told you that I had someone watching him, but you know you would have insisted on knowing why I was doing it," I said hoarsely. "Even if it wasn't him, I couldn't take that chance with your safety. Hell, maybe I should have told you my suspicions, but I wasn't sure you'd accept that theory. You were too close to the situation to see it. Hell, I had a hard time believing it, but it was the only thing that made sense to me after you told me he wanted to keep control of your finances."

B. A. Scott

"He's dead. He's guilty," she said in a shaky voice. "And I'm still having a hard time wrapping my head around the fact that he killed my parents. I thought he loved them as much as they loved him."

We arrived at her house, and I reached out the window to push in the code for the vehicle gate she'd given me earlier.

Her property was completely enclosed by a very tall, very sturdy fence, and she had extraordinary security, which had given me some peace of mind over the last several days.

I tipped the driver before I lifted Anna's shivering body out of the car and carried her into the house.

At that moment, I was glad the asshole who had killed her parents was already dead.

If he wasn't, I'd be tempted to make sure he never took another breath myself.

After everything that Anna had been through, she hadn't needed another painful blow like this one.

My only consolation was that I'd been here when she'd gotten that news, and I wasn't planning on leaving her anytime soon.

Anna was resilient, and she'd eventually get through the shock of Ray being her parents' murderer, but she was going to need time to absorb the truth.

She locked the door and reset the alarm system because my arms were full, and then I took her upstairs to her bedroom.

I'd familiarized myself with Anna's home before we'd left for the awards show.

I put her feet on the floor and got her out of that amazing dress and skimpy underwear before I shucked my own clothing. I carried her to the bed, covered both of us and wrapped her up in my arms to warm up her cold body.

She wrapped her arms around my warmer body and got as close to me as she could possibly get.

We stayed like that for a long time.

I wasn't going to push her to talk.

She had to deal with this in her own way.

"I don't want to think about this tonight," she whispered. "It was a good night, and you're here right now. I want you to know something."

"What, baby?" I said as I kissed the top of her head.

"I love you. Maybe it's too soon for me to say those words, but I think life is too short not to say them if they're in your heart."

I swallowed hard.

*Christ!* It was a shitty night for her, but she'd said the words I most wanted to hear from her lips.

"It's not too soon for me," I said, my voice hoarse with emotion from her revelation. "I love you, too, Anna. I think I have almost from the time we met and protecting you became my top priority. I wish I could protect you from this right now."

"You don't have to protect me anymore, Kaleb. Just love me. Make love to me. I'll think about everything else tomorrow."

Maybe I couldn't shield her from what she'd discovered tonight, but *that* I could definitely do.

## Chapter 31

*Anna*

Three months later, I nervously ran a hand through my hair as we walked down the driveway toward Wyatt and Shelby's home on the water in San Diego.

"Don't fuss," Kaleb said huskily. "You look beautiful."

I rolled my eyes. "You always say that."

"Because I'll always think you're beautiful, no matter what your hair looks like. And I think they're probably more nervous about meeting you than you are about meeting them."

I smiled at the usual response I always got from Kaleb to my comment. He was utterly predictable sometimes, but I loved his predictability.

My man was strong and steady, and his love for me was always there in his beautiful green eyes.

We'd spent the last three months flying back and forth between Los Angeles and Montana. We hadn't gone for more than a week without seeing each other because we couldn't last any longer than that.

I'd been back to Montana twice for a long weekend, but Kaleb usually came to me so we could do some of the things I'd never done in California because I'd always been too busy or on tour.

We'd gone to the theater, Disneyland, Universal Studios, The La Brea Tar Pits, Griffith Observatory, and multiple museums.

It had probably been the best three months of my entire life.

It had taken me a while to accept that Ray had killed my parents, but I was more at peace with their deaths now. The man who had killed them was dead.

Kaleb had gone to the cemetery near Bozeman with me because I'd needed to visit. I'd really needed to tell my parents how sorry I was that Ray had betrayed them, and I'd felt better after I'd spilled everything I was feeling at my parents' graves.

I wished that my mom and dad would have had the chance to meet Kaleb. I knew they would have loved him, and they would have loved the way that he loved me.

I didn't go on tour, and I'd hired a new agent who didn't push me to do anything I didn't want to do.

I was enjoying my summer, picking and choosing my appearances, and writing a lot of music about relationships and being in love for my new album.

I'd been totally inspired by my relationship with Kaleb.

Our relationship wasn't perfect, and it killed us to say goodbye so often, but we'd made it work because there was no other option.

We had to be together.

When he'd asked me to come to San Diego with him to meet his cousin and his best friend, I'd eagerly accepted.

I'd heard so much about both Wyatt and Shelby that I'd wanted to meet them.

I was nervous, as usual, because I knew they were both important to Kaleb.

He rang the doorbell.

The door flew open almost immediately and a pretty, curvy redhead threw herself into Kaleb's arms.

"Kaleb!" the woman squealed happily as he removed his arm from around my waist and hugged his cousin. "God, I've missed you so much."

"Let the poor man breathe, Shelby," a very large man said from behind her.

I was assuming this was Wyatt, and I was taken aback for a moment because he was even bigger and more muscular than Kaleb.

The man was intimidating, but the adoring look in his eyes when he looked at his wife obliterated some of his scariness.

Shelby stepped back and immediately pulled me into a sweet hug. "Anna, I've been looking forward to meeting you."

I hugged her back. The woman was so full of happiness and sunshine that I couldn't do anything else.

She put me immediately at ease.

Wyatt clapped Kaleb on the shoulder and put his hand out to me. "I second what Shelby just said. We've been looking forward to meeting the woman who could finally get Kaleb's attention. We just had no idea it would end up being a famous pop star."

I beamed at the big man as I shook his hand, and he grinned back at me.

Okay, maybe he wasn't *that* intimidating.

"Everyone, come in," Shelby requested as she opened the door wide and we trailed into the house. "I'm taking Anna into the kitchen with me. You guys can catch up in your office."

Wyatt lifted a brow. "I take it you'd like us to get lost while you two girl talk."

Shelby sent her husband a sweet smile and said bluntly, "Yes, please. Could you grab Kaleb a drink at the bar on your way to your office? I'll get Anna something in the kitchen."

"I'm on it," Wyatt said as he wandered to the bar with Kaleb behind him.

I followed Shelby into a beautiful gourmet kitchen, a room I knew that she loved because she was a chef.

Kaleb had shared a lot about his cousin, and I almost felt like I knew her.

"What can I get you to drink?" she asked politely.

I looked longingly at her very fancy coffee maker, one that was actually nicer than my own. "Would you mind if I asked for a coffee?"

"I can make you anything," she answered. "Do you have a preference?"

"A salted caramel latte if that's possible," I said hopefully.

She nodded like she served the drink on a daily basis and started to make the coffee. "That sounds good. I think I'll make the same for myself." She turned to me while she was working. "I won't keep us away from the guys for long, but I wanted a chance to tell you privately how sorry I am about your parents and everything that's happened to you. I lost both of my parents at the same time when I was a teenager. Car accident. I know how painful and traumatic it can be. It must have been heartbreaking for you to know that they were murdered by someone you thought was a friend. I just wanted you to know that if you ever need someone to talk to about it, I'll be there for you."

I took a seat at the breakfast bar because Shelby was obviously in her element and didn't need any help with those coffees. "Thanks," I said sincerely. "It's been a really tough year. I'm not sure what I would have done without Kaleb."

"I think you've been good for him, too," Shelby shared as she added a dash of salt and some whipped cream to the lattes. "I'm going to be honest. I was a little worried about him when I found out that he was getting involved with a huge celebrity like Annelise. But the more he and the family talked about you, I knew I was going to like you, too."

I wasn't even going to pretend that I didn't know what she was talking about. People on the outside of my business thought pop stars were materialistic, partying all the time, and incredibly narcissistic sometimes. While that was a fair assessment for some, there were people like me who just wanted to create music.

I wanted to reassure Shelby because she cared so much about Kaleb. "I love him. I'm not the party type. I'm actually pretty boring. Like your cousin, I was a complete workaholic who was obsessed with my career, and had no joy in my life. Kaleb brought that joy into my life, and I'd never hurt him."

Shelby slid my coffee in front of me with a spoon. She started stirring the whipped cream into her own mug as she said softly, "You've brought joy to Kaleb's life, too. I was worried about him because he blamed himself for my kidnapping for a long time, even though it wasn't his fault. We've always been close. He's more like a brother to me than a cousin. I could see the guilty look in his eyes every time he saw me after the kidnapping. I'm not seeing that anymore. He's sent me some of the pictures of you two seeing the sights in Southern California over the last few months. He looks so happy, and I don't think I can express how grateful I am about that."

Shelby looked like she was about to cry with gratitude, and that was the last thing I wanted. I reached across the breakfast bar and put a gentle hand on her forearm. "He's okay now, Shelby. You don't have to worry about that anymore. He's at peace with that situation and he's moved on."

"Because he has better things to worry about now. You."

I pulled my hand back and stirred my latte. "I'm working on that. He's an alpha male that tends to be a little too protective sometimes. I like that protective instinct, don't get me wrong. But I hate it that he worries."

Shelby sighed happily. "Wyatt is the same way. Over the top, and he's been worse since I was kidnapped. It's just part of who he is, and I try to remember that when it gets to be a little too much. I like his protectiveness, too, but when he gets unreasonable, I let him know."

"Same here," I shared as I decided that I really liked this woman. Shelby had a big heart, and I hadn't met many of those people in my world.

"How's the long-distance thing working out for you two?" she asked curiously.

"Honestly?" I asked. "It's hell. I miss him like crazy, but we don't really have a choice right now. His business is in Montana, and mine is in California. But anything is better than not having him in my life."

Shelby shook her head. "I don't know how you do it. Wyatt and I were apart for a short period of time when I was in Montana visiting, and it drove me insane. If he travels, I usually go with him because I hate being lonely at home. I can work remotely for the most part since I'm a food blogger and a writer of cookbooks now. Do you like Montana? Kaleb mentioned that you grew up there."

I nodded. "I love it. I love the town and most of the people there."

Shelby rolled her eyes. "I love it, too. But the gossip in Crystal Fork can be relentless."

I laughed. "Luckily, Kaleb lives outside of town, so it's always possible to escape when I want to. His property is beautiful. I feel a lot more inspired and peaceful there."

"Are you thinking about moving?" she asked curiously.

I shrugged. "Kaleb and I haven't really gone there. We love each other, but I'm not sure either of us knows what to do about the future."

"You'll figure it out," Shelby said confidently. "He could probably set up a remote office in Los Angeles."

"I'd never ask him to do that," I said, appalled. "He loves his family and the town he grew up in. He'd worry himself to death about his mom, even though Tanner and Devon are there."

Shelby nodded. "That's probably true. He's really been there for her since my uncle died. Aunt Millie and my uncle were inseparable when he was alive. She took his death really hard. Everyone did. You wouldn't know it, but I think she's really lonely."

I knew that. I'd sensed it when I was with her in Montana, and we still texted and spoke on the phone a lot.

"I miss her," I said honestly.

"Me, too," Shelby said. "I also miss her huckleberry pie."

I laughed. "She made a few for Kaleb and me. It was the best I've ever had. I crave it sometimes now."

"Would you miss California if you decided to move to Montana someday?" Shelby asked inquisitively.

I shook my head. "No. California is where my career is right now, but I've never really been a city girl."

"Then I guess a move is something you could think about in the future. You might still have to travel, but there are definitely benefits to being with a billionaire. They all have private jets."

*T. A. Scott*

Shelby changed the subject, probably because she didn't want me to think that she was pushing me to do something I wasn't ready to do yet.

We chatted a little more about anything and everything before we finally went to find our men.

# Chapter 32

*Kaleb*

I leaned against the wall of the shower enclosure as I recovered from getting myself off for about the millionth time in the last six weeks.

*Fuck!* It had been way too long since I'd seen Anna in person.

Six. Damn. Weeks.

The last time we'd spent together in person had been when we'd visited Wyatt and Shelby in San Diego for a few days.

Shelby and Anna had become fast friends, and I knew they texted and called each other fairly often.

She talked to Shelby almost as much as she spoke to my mother, and judging by the info my mother always had on Anna, they were rarely out of contact.

After we'd gone to San Diego, I'd had to fly to New York on business. I'd been really busy with a new acquisition.

After that situation had calmed down, Anna had been in long recording sessions in Los Angeles every single day for her new album.

I knew she'd put in those long days so she could finally get to Montana tonight. I'd balked at the time, but I was damn glad I was finally going to see her beautiful face about an hour or two from now.

B. A. Scott

I hadn't handled the long separation well.

Okay, to be totally honest, I'd been a major prick after the first week.

No doubt my brothers had to be ready to beg Anna to get here as quickly as possible.

If I'd wanted proof of how I could handle a long separation from Anna, the last six weeks had told me that being away from her for a long period of time was pure hell.

We had a running text conversation going, and we spoke on the phone at least once a day, but she'd sounded so damn tired from doing mega recording sessions that I hadn't kept her on the phone long.

I worried about her constantly.

She'd told me to call off my security once we'd found out who had murdered her parents. While I understood that she didn't want somebody following constantly, I didn't like the fact that no one was watching over her.

She was high profile, and there were so many crazy people out there who made it a priority to stalk women like Anna.

As far as I was concerned, she was never safe unless she was within my sight.

I'd given the situation a lot of thought, and I was more than ready to move to Los Angeles.

Yes, I'd miss my family, but I had a private jet that could get me home quickly if I needed to be here.

I could open an office in Los Angeles, or work remote.

I'd talked to Tanner and Devon, and they both supported my decision. Most likely because they couldn't stand to be around me anymore if Anna wasn't nearby.

Did I like the city life?

*Nope.*

I'd been there and done that in New York City years ago, and I'd been counting the days until I could move back to Montana.

New York City was way too crowded for a guy who liked his space.

I'd hated everything about that life except for the variety of food that could be had there.

However, the difference between New York City and Los Angeles is that New York City didn't have Anna Kendrick living and working there.

It wasn't just the more frequent sex that I missed.

I missed every damn thing about her.

Her smile.

Her laugh.

The way she handled details that I never even thought about.

The way she cared about everyone in this town.

The way she loved...me.

Anna had become my best friend, and I liked being able to tell her things that I'd never mention to another soul without worrying about her reaction to the weird stuff.

I fucking needed her.

I remembered wondering not that long ago how a man like Wyatt had been brought to his knees by Shelby.

Wyatt had been single and had planned on staying that way until he'd met Shelby.

Now, the two of them were happily married and inseparable.

I didn't wonder about how that had happened anymore.

I was well familiar with the insanity that took over a man's brain when they met the right woman.

I'd felt the same way Wyatt had felt before meeting Shelby.

I was the guy who didn't deal with complicated relationships, and I was probably in the most difficult relationship on the planet.

Grabbing my body wash, I started to clean up. I was extra careful to make sure I had the right container. I'd accidentally used some of the body wash Anna had left here one morning because I was distracted.

It was a moment I'd regretted because it had given off a faint scent that reminded me of Anna, and my dick had been hard all damn day.

I lathered up and started to get my ass in gear.

I'd have to leave for the airport in less than an hour because I wanted to make sure I was there when my jet landed.

I was anxious to see her face, but I already dreaded the goodbyes when it was time for her to leave again in a few days.

I turned off the shower, telling myself that I'd feel better once I had her close to me again, even if that time was limited.

I dried off and wrapped the towel around my waist so I could shave. That's when I heard a faint noise coming from the bedroom.

*My brothers?*

Nah, they never came up to my bedroom. They just bellowed from downstairs until I went down there to shut them up. Besides, they'd been in our office in Billings when I'd left a short time ago.

I opened the bathroom door, not sure what to expect.

It certainly wasn't anything I could have conjured up in my wildest dreams.

Anna was laying in the middle of the bed, completely naked, getting herself off, her head turned with her face in my pillow.

I watched, feeling like a creepy voyeur, but I couldn't help myself.

It was a scene out of my fantasies, and I sure as fuck wasn't going to shut it down.

I was mesmerized as I stepped a little closer to the bed, watching Anna satisfy herself with an enthusiasm that instantly got me rock hard.

She moaned as her fingers slid over her clit, again and again.

"Kaleb," she whimpered as her hips rose.

"Fuck!" I cursed softly.

Anna heard me and suddenly turned her head.

Our eyes met, and our gazes held as she suddenly stopped.

"Don't stop," I rasped.

She slowed her pace, but kept going.

"I was waiting for you to get out of the shower. The bed smells like you," she said in an aroused voice that made me half crazy.

I couldn't take my eyes away from hers.

"Is this what you do when we're not together?' I choked out.

"Yes," she confessed.

"Jesus, sweetheart, I think about this exact scene when I'm getting myself off. Keep going."

I wanted to palm my cock, but if I did, I'd explode again and probably be useless for a while.

Anna had never been shy about sex and her sexuality after our first time together, which was one of the things I fucking loved about her.

She was adventurous and open, and it didn't surprise me when she sped up her pace again.

"I always get myself off by pretending it's you with your head between my thighs," she said in a husky, fuck-me voice. "You always make me come so hard, Kaleb."

*Fucking hell!*

I was torn.

I was captivated as I watched her, but her words also made me want to dive onto the bed so I could taste her and finish that orgasm for her.

"Is that what you want?" I asked gruffly. "My head between your thighs?"

"Not necessarily," she panted. "Having you watch me is pretty hot, too. I'm ecstatic just to see you in person again."

I gave up. I dropped the towel and palmed my cock, my eyes never leaving the erotic sight on my bed.

I gritted my teeth and held back as Anna lost herself to her fantasy, her eyes hungry as she saw me stroking myself slowly, my eyes glued to *her.*

I knew the moment that she completely lost it.

Her eyes closed and she threw her head back, the hand that wasn't busy with her pussy plucking her nipples for extra stimulation.

"Kaleb!" she screamed as she started to climax.

*Christ!* She was beautiful when she was utterly consumed in her orgasm, and hearing her call my name while that was happening almost made me lose it.

I'd never had this kind of view, and it was going to be something I remembered when she wasn't here, and we weren't together.

I dove onto the bed as she was coming down, and positioned myself between her legs.

I surged inside her before she even had a chance to recover.

I knew I probably should have been patient, but my patience had been stretched until I finally snapped.

This woman was mine, and I couldn't wait another millisecond to claim her.

# Chapter 33

*Anna*

I took in a sharp breath as Kaleb buried his cock inside me. I wrapped my legs around his waist a second later.

I'd wanted this, I'd wanted him for so long that the pleasure was nearly unbearable.

I'd missed Kaleb so much, and being this close to him again was nearly more than I could take.

"Oh, God," I whimpered. "You feel so good."

His strokes were fast, deep, and completely uncontrolled.

My hips rose to meet every thrust, relishing his wildness as he claimed me, heart and soul.

After the way that I teased him, I knew this wouldn't last long, but I was going to savor every second of his frenzied possession.

He felt amazing.

He smelled incredible.

And just the fact that our bodies were skin-to-skin again after being apart for so long was pure ecstasy.

"I love you," I said breathlessly as I ground my hips up against him.

"I love you, too," he growled. "You're mine, Anna. Say it. I fucking need to hear it after not seeing you for so damn long."

"I'll always be yours, Kaleb, and you'll always be mine, even when we're not physically in the same place."

He grasped my ass and pulled me up harder as his pace got so fast that I couldn't keep up.

He moved slightly until I had maximum stimulation to my clit, and I felt my climax building...again.

Kaleb never allowed himself to find his own release unless I came with him.

I sank my nails into his back because the pleasure was so intense when I finally began to orgasm harder than I had when I was masturbating.

"Kaleb!" I called out, almost afraid of the power of this particular climax.

And then, I let go, knowing Kaleb would be there to catch me when I came down again.

My core clenched down hard around his cock.

"I love you," I said mindlessly. "I missed you so much."

"Fuck! I love you, too, Anna," Kaleb said with a low, feral groan as he found his own release.

He rolled, our bodies still locked together as I rested on top of him.

It took a moment for my heart rate to slow down.

"Why don't you just fucking marry me and put me out of my misery," Kaleb said huskily near my ear. "I'll happily move to California if that means we can live together in the same place. The last six weeks had been pure hell."

Tears formed in my eyes as I whispered, "You'd actually move to California to be with me?"

Even though we were locked in post coital bliss, I was pretty sure that he was dead serious, and knew exactly what he was asking.

He wanted to marry me, and he was willing to move to California and give up everything he had here...for me.

"There's nothing I wouldn't do for you, Anna," he answered. "Please put me out of my misery and marry me."

My heart tripped. "Is that an official proposal?"

"Yes, dammit!" he growled. "This wasn't the way I planned on asking you to spend the rest of your life with me, but it seems that

B. A. Scott

I have no finesse when it comes to you. I missed being with you for
your thirty-sixth birthday, and I want that to be the last event in
your life that I miss. I already have your engagement ring. I'd just
rather you didn't move at the moment. I haven't been this close to
you in a long time."

A tear escaped from my eye. "Yes. My answer is *yes* to your proposal. You sent a ridiculous number of gifts to me for my birthday,
and a birthday cake."

"It's not the same as being there with you in person," he grumbled.

I'd hoped that he'd propose to me someday, but I hadn't wanted
to get my hopes up, and I really hadn't expected it to happen *today*.

I'd known for a while now that I wanted to marry Kaleb and be
with him for the rest of my life.

"However," I continued. "There's no reason for you to move to
California unless you want to do the long-distance thing again. I'm
staying here, Kaleb. My parents' house has sold already, and I put
mine up for sale right before I left. I brought a ridiculous amount
of things with me, and the rest of my personal things are in storage
waiting to be shipped here."

"What about your career, Anna?" he said, concerned. "I want
you to be happy."

"I am happy. Happier than I've been in my entire life. I'm going to
arrange to build a recording studio in Billings," I told him. "There's
nothing I can't do here except for personal appearances. I'll still have
to travel some, but I'm not doing mega tours anymore. At least not in
the foreseeable future. It made me miserable, even before I met you."

"Thank fuck!" Kaleb cursed. "If you wanted to tour, I would have
gone with you, at least for a portion of your tour, and it kills me to
see you so uptight that you throw up."

"I'm a little tired of that myself," I said, amused. "I'd much rather
focus on writing music for myself and for other artists. It makes
me happy. Being in Crystal Fork makes me happy. You, Kaleb
Remington, make me *incredibly* happy."

He wrapped his arms a little tighter around my body. "I can't
believe you're going to move here for me."

I was miserable without you, too, Anna. My brothers will be glad you're here to stay. I've been a major asshole to everyone."

"Feeling better?" I joked.

"What do you think?" he asked drily. "You're here. You're not leaving, and you're going to marry me. I'm probably the happiest asshole on the planet right now."

I sighed as I made circles on Kaleb's shoulder with my index finger.

I knew I should roll off his warm body, but truthfully, there was nothing better than being naked with him like this.

I liked the intimacy of being skin-to-skin with him. It was going to take me a while to realize that we were finally together and that neither of us were going anywhere anytime soon.

Kaleb was the first to break our contact.

He gently rolled me over, disentangled our tangled bodies, and got out of bed.

"Where are you going?" I asked.

"Disappointed?" he said with a wicked look on his face.

"Yes," I admitted.

"Don't go anywhere," he said in a bossy tone. "Give me a few seconds."

He went to his walk-in closet and returned in just over a few seconds later.

"I decided I needed to see my ring on your finger right now," he told me as he got back into bed.

I sat up as he handed me a gorgeous velvet box.

"I'm going to ask that question again," he cautioned me. "Marry me, Anna?"

My hands trembled and my heart was beating out of my chest as I popped the lid of the box open.

It didn't surprise me that it was the most beautiful ring I'd ever seen.

Kaleb had exquisite taste when it came to jewelry.

The band was platinum since Kaleb already knew that I rarely wore yellow gold. There were a ridiculous amount of diamonds in the gorgeous ring, and the quality of the diamonds were spectacular.

There was a beautiful solitaire in the middle, surrounded by smaller stones.

"I didn't want to get anything too big so you can wear it while you're playing the piano," Kaleb explained.

"Is this honestly what you'd call a small ring?" I teased.

"Compared to what I wanted to get you, yeah, it's a reasonable size."

I smiled. I guessed that maybe he *had* compromised. "It's perfect," I told him softly, still in awe of the gorgeous ring he'd chosen.

I liked unique jewelry, and this ring was a work of art.

"Are you ever going to answer my question?" he asked impatiently as he took the ring back from me and removed it from the box.

I crooked a brow. "Yes, you know I'm going to marry you. I'm a sure thing for you, too, handsome."

He grinned as he put the ring on my finger.

It fit perfectly.

I held my hand out to admire the way the diamonds flashed on my finger.

And just like that...Kaleb Remington and I were officially engaged.

Kaleb frowned. "I guess you're probably not going to want to change your last name. Everyone knows you as Annelise Kendrick."

"Then I'll officially be Annelise Kendrick Remington. Everyone simply thinks of me as Annelise unless they know me personally. I'll be Anna Remington to anyone who knows me."

I *wanted* to be part of the Remington family, which included taking Kaleb's last name. Any children we had would be Remingtons, too.

Kaleb tossed the ring box on the side table, laid down on his back, and pulled me back on top of him again. "Now where were we?" he asked in a sexy baritone. "I think I was about to make up for that very brief encounter a little while ago."

"Were you?" I purred as I straddled him.

Maybe it had been briefer than usual, but we'd both needed it that way.

We'd been apart for way too long, and it hadn't taken me long to go off for a second time.

I leaned down and kissed him.

He returned that embrace with a thoroughness that took my breath away.

"I'm not in a hurry this time," he promised me. "Ride me, beautiful. Take what you need this time."

I'd taken what I needed last time, but I wasn't about to argue if Kaleb was giving me control.

We both took what we wanted, finally knowing that the act was a promise of forever for both of us.

## Epilogue

*Anna*

*Two Weeks Later…*

Kaleb and I were married two weeks after he'd proposed in a small church in Crystal Fork.

I'd been flabbergasted when he'd named a date.

I'd told him it couldn't be done in two weeks, even though I'd had no real objection to the date.

He'd proved me wrong. With friends and family pitching in, the details and the work had been accomplished very quickly.

I hadn't minded being wrong. I was as eager as he was to get on with the rest of our lives because we had so many plans for our future.

The service had been relatively small because there wasn't enough space for the whole town to cram into that chapel.

Wyatt, Tanner, and Devon had stood up for Kaleb.

Kim had been my matron of honor, and I'd asked Shelby to be my bridesmaid.

Although the wedding had been smaller and cozy, the reception was massive. Most of the town *was* in attendance.

Millie had asked to host the reception at her place since she loved planning parties and events at her home.

Kaleb had readily accepted because that meant he didn't have to do cleanup duty before he took me away for our honeymoon in Italy.

He had, however, gotten the event catered so we didn't have to deal with the massive amount of food that was needed to feed most of the town.

We'd set up classy tents that were heated, but they really hadn't been necessary. It was a lovely fall day and much warmer than what was usual for this time of year in Montana.

"Did I happen to tell you how beautiful you look today?" Kaleb asked from his place beside me at the table.

I turned to look at him, resplendent in a formal tuxedo.

Our wedding party was seated around us outside at the big table, all of us eating the delicious food from the caterer.

Honestly, I felt beautiful.

I'd opted to go with an ivory wedding dress instead of stark white because bright white was definitely not my color. It had a blush lining so the details of the dress popped. The train was short, and I loved the fitted lace sleeves. After the dress was chosen, it was quickly tailored to fit me perfectly.

Kim had done my hair, and I'd ditched the traditional veil and went with some artfully placed pearl combs that matched my dress.

Kaleb had told me that I looked beautiful many times today, but the covetous look in his gorgeous green eyes sent a shiver of awareness down my spine.

"Many times," I finally answered. "But thank you...again. You look extremely handsome yourself."

Kaleb in formal wear took my breath away...always.

It wasn't just the tuxedo that made me breathless, it was the way he could wear it without looking the least bit uncomfortable.

Being a billionaire businessman, he'd probably needed to go black tie many times in the past.

"I know you're missing your own parents today. I'm sorry, sweetheart," Kaleb said in a deep, quiet voice.

I did miss my parents, but the pain was bearable now.

I wished that they could be here, but I hadn't let those clouds overshadow the happiest day of my life.

"They would have loved you, your mother, and your family. Are you missing your dad?"

"A little," he admitted as he put his fork on his empty plate. "I wished you two could have met, but I'm not any less happy today because of it."

"I feel that way, too. I can't believe we're married. It happened so fast that I haven't had time to think about how it would feel once the ceremony was over."

"And how do you feel?" Kaleb questioned.

"Like I'm doing exactly what I want and that I'm exactly where I belong," I said honestly. "What about you?"

I wasn't sure how to put my emotions into words, but that something inside me that had never felt quite right had finally settled into place.

"When we met, I was restless," he admitted. "Something was missing from my life, and now I know exactly what was missing. It was *you*, Anna. You were the one thing I needed that all of my money couldn't buy."

I put my hand on his muscular thigh, and he covered that hand with his own.

Sometimes, Kaleb and I didn't really need the words. We understood each other.

Maybe we'd been searching for the same thing, but we'd been so many miles apart that we hadn't been able to find each other.

I'd probably never believe that fate hadn't sent me down the wrong driveway and to his mother's cabin that day, and I was a firm believer that a person made their own destiny.

Something had been drawing me to Montana after I'd had that meltdown.

I could have gone a hundred different places to find my solitude.

But, as fate would have it, I'd finally ended up in the same place as Kaleb.

What were the chances of that happening on its own?

He squeezed my hand. "I think I'm about ready to sweep my bride away."

I was so startled that I giggled. "We can't. We haven't even cut that beautiful cake. You can't possibly want me naked right now. You should be exhausted after the last two weeks."

We'd made up for all the lost time we'd spent apart, and then some.

Kaleb caught my gaze as he said, "There is *never* going to be a time when I won't want you, Anna, but I suppose I can wait a little longer."

He sounded so disgruntled that I shot him a naughty smile before I said, "I'll make it worth your while."

His expression was intense as he held my gaze. "Just being with you, right here and right now, is enough for me, Anna. This feels like a fucking miracle to me."

Tears formed in my eyes, but I blinked them back so I didn't have mascara running down my face.

This man was a dream come true for me, too.

I had no doubt that we'd disagree sometimes.

Neither of us were perfect.

But we were perfect together.

I leaned close to him. "I wrote a song for you. I want to play it for you when we get back home. I need to be at the piano. It's our story. It might sound a little bit crazy because I know you don't believe in fate."

"I think I've changed my mind about that since I met you," he said with a grin. "Now I'm really eager to get home."

"Cake first, and then I'm getting my first dance with my gorgeous new husband."

Devon had taken care of the music. He was playing with a local band, and a dance floor had already been set up.

"It's your day, sweetheart. As long as you're smiling and safe, I'm happy."

God, I loved that about him. He was always trying to please me, which made me want to do the same for him.

Kaleb's happiness meant the world to me.

"When are you cutting that cake?" Devon asked from across the table. "I think everyone is done eating. Ever since I heard about it, I've wanted to eat that cake."

The cake wasn't very traditional. It was still beautiful, but I'd gone strictly for taste. It was a combination of flavors, including chunks of fudge and Belgian chocolate mixed in, and of course, some caramel.

"We'll do it when we feel like it," Kaleb said nonchalantly, deliberately stalling because he knew Devon wanted that cake right now.

Tanner leaned closer to his younger brother and said something inaudible.

Knowing Tanner, he was probably telling his little brother that it was Kaleb's day, and not to be a pain in the ass.

"There's something else that I'd much rather see than those two cutting the cake," Kaleb's mother said with a mischievous smile.

"What?" Devon asked, disgruntled.

Millie picked up her spoon and lightly began to tap her glass as a signal for Kaleb and me to kiss.

A moment later, others joined her.

Kaleb stretched his arm across the back of my chair, and I looked up at him with a smile.

"I've always hated this stupid, noisy tradition until today," he said gruffly, loud enough to be heard over the noise.

"Me, too," I agreed as I looked into his eyes.

We both leaned in and our lips met.

I was planning on a short embrace, but Kaleb palmed the back of neck and held his mouth to mine.

It wasn't a carnal or sexual kiss.

It was a solemn promise to love each other for the rest of our lives.

For a moment, I forgot there was anyone else near us because I was so captivated and moved by the embrace.

I twined my arms around his neck, and the kiss went on way longer than it should have.

Neither of us were in any hurry.

It was a moment to savor and celebrate.

After everything we'd been through together, this grieving, confused pop star and my restless, workaholic billionaire had *finally* found our way to our happily ever after.

I'd finally found joy in my life, and I'd never have to say goodbye to *him* again.

~*The End*~

Please visit me at:
http://www.authorjsscott.com
http://www.facebook.com/authorjsscott

You can write to me at
jsscott_author@hotmail.com

You can also tweet
@AuthorJSScott

Please sign up for my Newsletter for updates,
new releases and exclusive excerpts.

## Books by J. S. Scott:

### Billionaire Obsession Series

The Billionaire's Obsession~Simon
Heart of the Billionaire
The Billionaire's Salvation
The Billionaire's Game
Billionaire Undone~Travis
Billionaire Unmasked~Jason
Billionaire Untamed~Tate
Billionaire Unbound~Chloe
Billionaire Undaunted~Zane
Billionaire Unknown~Blake
Billionaire Unveiled~Marcus
Billionaire Unloved~Jett
Billionaire Unwed~Zeke
Billionaire Unchallenged~Carter
Billionaire Unattainable~Mason
Billionaire Undercover~Hudson

Billionaire Unexpected~Jax
Billionaire Unnoticed~Cooper
Billionaire Unclaimed~Chase
Billionaire Unreachable~Wyatt
Billionaire Unexplained~Kaleb
Billionaire Unforgettable~ Tanner

## British Billionaires Series

Tell Me You're Mine
Tell Me I'm Yours
Tell Me This Is Forever

## Sinclair Series

The Billionaire's Christmas
No Ordinary Billionaire
The Forbidden Billionaire
The Billionaire's Touch
The Billionaire's Voice
The Billionaire Takes All
The Billionaire's Secret
Only A Millionaire

## Accidental Billionaires

Ensnared
Entangled
Enamored
Enchanted
Endeared

## Walker Brothers Series

Release
Player
Damaged

## The Sentinel Demons

The Sentinel Demons: The Complete Collection
A Dangerous Bargain
A Dangerous Hunger
A Dangerous Fury
A Dangerous Demon King

### The Vampire Coalition Series

The Vampire Coalition: The Complete Collection
The Rough Mating of a Vampire (Prelude)
Ethan's Mate
Rory's Mate
Nathan's Mate
Liam's Mate
Daric's Mate

### Changeling Encounters Series

Changeling Encounters: The Complete Collection
Mate Of The Werewolf
The Dangers Of Adopting A Werewolf
All I Want For Christmas Is A Werewolf

### The Pleasures of His Punishment

The Pleasures of His Punishment: The Complete Collection
The Billionaire Next Door
The Millionaire and the Librarian
Riding with the Cop
Secret Desires of the Counselor
In Trouble with the Boss
Rough Ride with a Cowboy
Rough Day for the Teacher
A Forfeit for a Cowboy
Just what the Doctor Ordered
Wicked Romance of a Vampire

### The Curve Collection: Big Girls and Bad Boys Series

The Curve Collection: The Complete Collection
The Curve Ball
The Beast Loves Curves
Curves by Design

### Writing as Lane Parker

Dearest Stalker
Dearest Protector
A Christmas Dream
A Valentine's Dream
Lost: A Mountain Man Rescue Romance

*A Dark Horse Novel w/ Cali MacKay*
Bound
Hacked

## *Taken By A Trillionaire Series*
Virgin for the Trillionaire by Ruth Cardello
Virgin for the Prince by J.S. Scott
Virgin to Conquer by Melody Anne
Prince Bryan: Taken By A Trillionaire

## *Other Titles*
Well Played w/Ruth Cardello

Made in the USA
Columbia, SC
14 May 2024

35376378R00155